Aunt Dimity
Beats the Devil

VIKING
75 years
•

also by Nancy Atherton

AUNT DIMITY'S DEATH ⸺ AUNT DIMITY AND THE DUKE
AUNT DIMITY'S GOOD DEED ⸺ AUNT DIMITY DIGS IN
AUNT DIMITY'S CHRISTMAS

Aunt Dimity
Beats the Devil

NANCY ATHERTON

VIKING

VIKING

Published by the Penguin Group

Penguin Putnam Inc., 375 Hudson Street, New York, New York 10014, U.S.A.

Penguin Books Ltd, 27 Wrights Lane, London W8 5TZ, England

Penguin Books Australia Ltd, Ringwood, Victoria, Australia

Penguin Books Canada Ltd, 10 Alcorn Avenue, Toronto, Ontario, Canada M4V 3B2

Penguin Books (N.Z.) Ltd, 182–190 Wairau Road, Auckland 10, New Zealand

Penguin Books Ltd, Registered Offices:
Harmondsworth, Middlesex, England

First published in 2000 by Viking Penguin,
a member of Penguin Putnam Inc.

1   3   5   7   9   10   8   6   4   2

PUBLISHER'S NOTE

This is a work of fiction. Names, characters, places, and incidents either are the product
of the author's imagination or are used fictitiously, and any resemblance to actual per-
sons, living or dead, business establishments, events, or locales is entirely coincidental.

Library of Congress Cataloging-in-Publication Data
Atherton, Nancy.
Aunt Dimity beats the devil/Nancy Atherton.
p.   cm.
ISBN 0-670-89179-7
1. Dimity, Aunt (Fictitious character)—Fiction.   2. Women detectives—
England—Cornwall (County)—Fiction.   3. Cornwall (England: County)—
Fiction.   I. Title.

PS3551.T426 A934 2000
813'.54—dc21   00-034965

This book is printed on acid-free paper.
∞

Printed in the United States of America
Set in Perpetua
Designed by Lorelle Graffeo

Aunt Dimity
Beats the Devil

CHAPTER

1

It was a dark and stormy afternoon on the high moors of Northumberland. A cold October rain battered the Range Rover's roof and the fog was as thick as porridge. I hoped my hosts at Wyrdhurst Hall would hold high tea for me, because it looked as though I might be a bit late.

Thanks to the murky weather, I'd almost certainly missed the turnoff for Wyrdhurst's gated drive. To judge by the Rover's lurching progress, I'd somehow left the paved road altogether and veered onto a narrow, muddy track that seemed to be climbing straight into the clouds.

I could do nothing but climb with it. The moorland rose steeply to my right and fell sharply to my left. There was no place to turn around and I had no intention of backing down a road I could barely see.

I had even less intention of using my handy cell phone to

inform my husband of the vehicular pickle I'd gotten myself into. Bill had already expressed grave reservations about my ability to drive without incident from our home in the Cotswolds to a remote location near the Scottish border. If I called to tell him where I was—or more precisely, where I wasn't—he wouldn't say "I told you so," but he'd think it loudly enough for me to hear.

Apart from that, there was nothing Bill could do to help, short of sending a Hercules helicopter to airlift me to safety, and I couldn't imagine even the most intrepid chopper pilot volunteering to fly in such wretched weather.

The only phone call I was tempted to make was a transatlantic one to Boston, to pour my frustration into the ear of Dr. Stanford J. Finderman, my former boss. The farther I climbed, the more willing I was to blame Stan for every splash of rain that blurred my windshield. After all, the trip had been his idea. I ground my teeth as I recalled the way in which he'd goaded me into driving to a distant corner of northeastern England in the monsoon month of October.

"Shepherd! How the hell are ya?" Stan was the curator of my alma mater's rare-book collection, but his colorful language owed more to a stint in the navy than to his years in the rarefied world of rare books. "You remember Dickie Byrd?"

I shook the cobwebs from my professional memory and came up with: Richard Fleetwood Byrd; head of a thriving family firm based in northern England; a hardnosed, irascible rascal with a soft spot for illuminated manuscripts. I hadn't laid eyes on him for the past eight years, but I doubted that he'd changed much since then.

"The scrap-iron king of Newcastle?" I sat at the desk in the study, where I'd taken the call. "Sure, I remember him. What's up with Dickie?"

"His niece Nicole just got married," Stan informed me. "Goes by the name Nicole Hollander now. Hubby's called Jared."

"You want me to drop off a wedding present?" I asked.

"Just listen up, will ya?" Stan replied testily. "Dickie's Nicole's legal guardian and she's the apple of his eye. Little Nickie wanted a country house for a wedding present, so Dickie let her choose one of the family estates. She chose a big old Victorian heap way the hell up in Northumberland. It's called Wyrdhurst Hall."

"Weird hearse?" I echoed, grimacing. "Creepy name for a wedding present."

"Dust off your Old English dictionary, Shepherd. It's spelled W-Y-R-D-H-U-R-S-T. Means 'watch-place on the wooded hill.' Dickie's grandpa built it. Came complete with its own library—more than a thousand books, Dickie tells me."

"Now, *that's* a nice wedding present," I observed.

"I thought so, too," Stan agreed, "but Dickie doesn't think the books in the library are classy enough for his princess. Wants a professional to decide whether to keep 'em or replace 'em with something better. I'd go myself, but I've got to chair a frigging conservation conference at Yale. Besides, my department's budget . . ."

"Yeah, yeah, yeah," I muttered. I'd heard it all before. Whenever Stan caught the scent of a book deal in England, he called on me to check it out. My old boss seemed to be under the impression that I'd moved my family from Boston to a tiny Cotswolds village for the sole purpose of stretching his travel budget. "What's Dickie offering in return for our services?"

"The Serenissima," Stan replied.

I gave a low whistle. The Serenissima was a fifteenth-century prayer book adorned with gold leaf, semiprecious stones, and lots of bright enamel. It was the kind of thing Stan could show off proudly at donors' dinners. "Isn't that a pretty big payoff for such a little favor?"

"What can I say? Dickie wants the best bookman in the business to work for his niece. That's why he called me. And that's why I'm calling you. Will ya help me out, Shepherd? Northumberland's right up your alley—all the scenery you can eat."

I was tempted, sorely tempted, by Stan's offer. It had been ages since I'd prowled a really juicy private library, and I'd never set foot in Northumberland. The Gypsy in me kicked up her heels at the thought of roaming those misty, myth-filled hills, but the responsible mother in me put her foot down.

"How long will it take?" I asked.

"A week, tops," Stan assured me. "The Hollanders are already in residence. They'll put you up in style."

"A week?" I sighed. "That's an awfully long time for me to be away. Bill might not want to spend a whole week on his own with the twins, now that they're walking and talking and teething and—"

"Your new nanny a stinker?" Stan interrupted.

My new nanny was, in fact, worth more to me than the Serenissima would ever be. Annelise Sciaparelli had inherited the job from her older sister, who'd married and moved to Oxford. Childminding skills evidently ran in the family, because Annelise was every bit as caring and competent as Francesca had been.

"Annelise is a gem," I replied, "but—"

"When's the last time Bill hightailed it off on one of his business trips?" Stan pressed. "What's sauce for the goose . . ."

"That's unfair," I protested. "Bill's work is important and—"

"And yours isn't? I get the picture, Shepherd. Just let me know what your lord and master decides, will ya?" My old boss snorted derisively and hung up.

I returned the phone to its cradle and gazed pensively through the study's ivy-webbed window. I should have ignored Stan's cheap shots, treated them with the contempt they deserved, and I would have, if they hadn't contained one tiny particle of truth.

I hadn't gotten out much, lately, whereas Bill had gotten out quite a lot.

In the nineteen months since the twins had been born, I'd spent exactly one night apart from them. Bill, on the other hand, had been gone for weeks on end, supervising the European branch of his family's law firm. I'd agreed to the arrangement willingly enough—no job was more important to me than motherhood—but Stan's pointed comments made it seem a smidge unfair.

It certainly wasn't healthy. Will and Rob were pearls beyond price, but after a year and a half in their company, I was beginning to sink to their level. As proof, I recalled a fifth-wedding-anniversary dinner at a swanky restaurant in Oxford. Neither Bill nor I would ever forget the pained look on the sommelier's face when I sipped the wine, grimaced horribly, and declared it "yucky."

Clearly, my brain was stagnating. I needed to spend more time among grownups, for the sake of my vocabulary, if nothing else.

While the mother in me dithered, the Gypsy danced, stirred by the lure of those misty hills. By the time I sat down to discuss the trip with my husband, the Gypsy had won out.

"Bill," I began with steely determination, "Stan has a project for me, up in Northumberland."

"That's great!" Bill exclaimed. "It'll do you a world of good to get away from the cottage for a while, and frankly, I'd love to spend some time alone with the boys. I don't want them to grow up thinking fatherhood's a part-time job."

"B-but I'll be gone for at least a week," I sputtered, disconcerted by Bill's support. It was like slamming a fist into a pile of whipped cream.

"No problem," said Bill. "I'll rearrange my schedule, and Gerald can take care of any urgent business that comes up. With Annelise on hand to help with the boys, there'll be nothing for you to worry about."

"True," I acknowledged weakly.

"I can join you when you've finished the job," Bill enthused. "We'll drive up to Edinburgh together and take in a session of the new Scottish Parliament. I've been wanting to see it in action. It's the first time in nearly three hundred years that the Scots——" He broke off in midstream to eye me curiously. "For heaven's sake, Lori, you don't have to ask my permission to go. Who do you think I am? Your lord and master?"

"I think," I said, melting, "you're just about perfect."

After kissing my husband as thoroughly as I knew how, I picked up the phone to call Stan, who was tickled pink by the news.

"Knew I could count on you, Shepherd. I'll fax the details and let the Hollanders know you're on your way. Enjoy the scenery."

What scenery? I fumed as the Range Rover continued its precarious ascent. I couldn't see much farther than the white knuckles of my hands gripping the steering wheel. The weatherman on the car radio informed me cheerfully that it had been raining heavily in the north for the past month and seemed to suggest that it would go on raining well into the foreseeable future. I hoped the sun had shone on the Hollanders' wedding day, because I was willing to bet they hadn't seen it since.

There was no point in blaming Stan for my predicament. He might have goaded me into going to Northumberland, but he hadn't made it rain, so I left the cell phone in my shoulder bag, beneath the jacket I'd tossed on the passenger's seat.

Something small and pebbly bounced off the Rover's roof. "Hail," I muttered, rolling my eyes. "What's next? Locusts?"

I glanced over my shoulder at the spots usually occupied by the twins' safety seats, thanked heaven that my boys were safe at home, and nearly swerved off the road as a shower of rocks smacked into the Rover, cracking the windshield and splintering the side windows into a million jagged shards. Scared witless, I jammed on the brakes and skidded to the brink of a landslide that had obliterated the muddy track.

Even as I watched, a spitting, roiling cataract crashed down the steep hillside, devouring the narrow lane and sweeping debris down into the mist. Gingerly, I reached for the gear lever, to shift into reverse, but before I could get hold of it, the car gave a sickening shudder and tilted crazily toward the churning torrent. The ground was giving way beneath my wheels.

My hand froze in midair, then returned slowly, carefully, to release the seat belt. Scarcely daring to breathe, I reached for the door handle, nudged the door open with my elbow, and flung myself onto the muddy track, where blind panic sent me scrambling away from the precipice. Panting with fear, I swung around just in time to see the Range Rover turn tail-up and plunge, like a breaching whale, into the fog-bound valley.

I sank limply into the mud, choking back terrified sobs while a tiny, rational corner of my brain stood back calmly and took stock of my situation.

No car, no phone, no coat, and no umbrella. No broken bones, granted, but also no idea of where I was or where I might find shelter.

High tea at Wyrdhurst Hall was looking iffy.

CHAPTER

I was so cold I'd stopped shivering. My rain-soaked sweater hung nearly to my knees, my wool trousers clung to my legs like rotting leaves, and my suede boots oozed mud as I staggered forward, buffeted by a bone-chilling gust. The wind seemed to gain strength as my own failed.

Still, I kept walking, numbed in mind as well as body, unable to recall where I was or how I'd gotten there, knowing only that if I stopped moving I'd die.

And I couldn't allow that to happen. Will and Rob were waiting for me, just beyond the next bend, and Bill was right there with them. They had warm clothes for me, a hot meal, and a fluffy comforter big enough for us all. I'd made it down the muddy track to the paved road, hadn't I? Surely I could make it to the next bend.

If only the heather weren't so alluring. If only I could resist the urge to curl up on the springy turf and fall asleep. Just a short nap, that's all I wanted. The boys would understand. They wouldn't want Mummy to be so very, very tired.

A sharp rap to my right kneecap nearly knocked me over. Looking down, I saw that I'd walked straight into a low wall by the side of the road. Beyond the wall, like a humble Camelot rising from Avalon's mists, stood a tiny white-washed cottage with two deepset windows and a peacock-blue front door. Smoke curled from its chimney only to be shredded by the grasping wind. I watched the curling smoke, mesmerized, until Bill ordered me to snap out of it. Vision blurring, I stumbled feebly to the blue door, raised a frozen fist, and pounded twice.

"Please," I whispered, felt my legs fold beneath me, and slumped, senseless, to the ground.

I swam lazily through an endless ocean of sleep, vaguely aware of the acrid scent of burning coal, the flicker of firelight on my eyelids, and the familiar pressure of Bill's body nestled close to mine beneath a thick layer of soft blankets. Eyes closed, reluctant to rise from the bottomless depths of slumber, I turned my head to nuzzle the crook of his neck.

"Mmm," I murmured. "You're warm."

"That was the general idea," said a voice.

The voice did not seem to be my husband's.

"Bill?" I ventured hopefully.

"No Bill here, I'm afraid," said the voice. "Will an Adam do?"

I opened my eyes and found myself staring at a not unat-
tractive but wholly unfamiliar collarbone. When I lifted my
gaze, I saw a tousle of black curls framing a pale, heart-shaped
face I'd never seen before. The stranger's eyes, dark as a
Gypsy's, sparkled like wine in the firelight and his lips were
close enough to graze my brow.

"Adam Chase, at your service," he said, his breath ruffling
my hair. "And you would be?"

"Lori," I croaked. "Lori Shepherd."

"I don't usually object to women falling into my arms,
Lori Shepherd, but you gave me quite a fright." Adam Chase
propped himself up on his elbow, taking care to tuck the
blankets in between us. His action underscored the interesting
fact that we were both as naked as guppies. Confusion must
have suffused my face because he added, "Body heat. It was
the only way I could think to thaw you."

"Oh," I said, at a loss. "Thank you."

"Not at all," said Adam. "Do you think you could manage
a bit of broth?"

My stomach, as if on cue, rumbled. "I was supposed to
take high tea at Wyrdhurst," I murmured dazedly.

"Were you? What a pity. It's well past teatime now."
Adam swung his legs over the side of the narrow iron bed
and contrived to pull on a pair of black jeans without revealing more than an inch or two of lean, well-muscled haunch.
He reached for a black sweatshirt that had been slung over
the back of a worn brown leather armchair and held it out
to me.

"Your clothes aren't dry and I don't want you to take a
chill." He hesitated. "Can you dress yourself or shall I——"

"I can manage," I blurted, then blushed, embarrassed by my overreaction. It wasn't as if my rescuer would see anything he hadn't seen already.

Adam seemed to understand. "Of course," he said gravely, as I took the sweatshirt from him. "If you need me, I'll be in the kitchen."

His parting words were slightly facetious, because there was no kitchen, as such. Once I'd hauled myself into a sitting position and drawn the sweatshirt well past my hips, I saw that the cottage was nothing more than one large room, its sections defined by furnishings rather than walls.

The kitchen corner featured a wall-mounted cupboard above a stone sink with a single spigot. Beside the sink, a pine countertop held a pair of gas rings, a cutting board, and a clay flowerpot bristling with utensils.

A modest pine table and a pair of beechwood chairs made up the dining room. Above the pine table hung a brass oil lamp, which Adam lit on his way to the kitchen.

The area to the right of the front door had been set up as an office, with a five-drawer kneehole desk, a swivel chair, and a pair of heavy-laden bookcases. The desk held a portable typewriter, miscellaneous papers, and a jam jar filled with pens and colored pencils.

The corner opposite the office must have served as the bedroom. Shirts hung from pegs above a small chest of drawers, and a nightstand stood beside an empty space where the iron bed would have stood if it hadn't been pushed close to the fireplace, for my benefit. The leather armchair, and the ottoman that went with it, had been thrust from their traditional spots before the hearth to make room for the bed.

My clothes—all of them—dangled from the edge of the

simple plank mantelpiece, anchored there by a row of smooth, fist-sized stones. My suede boots sat at a little distance from the fire, where they would dry without splitting. They'd be stiff by morning, though, thanks to the mud.

"We're a bit isolated here." A match flared and Adam bent low to light the gas rings. He placed a saucepan on one, a teakettle on the other. "I've no telephone, and my car is in the village at the moment, undergoing repairs. I've a bicycle"—he motioned toward a sturdy mountain bike leaning just inside the front door—"so I could have ridden into town for help, but I didn't want to leave you alone."

As he stirred the contents of the saucepan, a series of fuzzy images took shape in my mind—gray fog, silver rain, and a muddy brown track swept away by a savage torrent.

"The only thing left," Adam was saying, "was to build up the fire and sandwich you between its warmth and mine." He lifted a spoonful of soup to his lips. "Purely for medicinal purposes, you understand."

I felt the cold rain soak my sweater as the Range Rover sank from view, and shuddered violently.

"My God," I whispered, shrinking back against the pillows.

The spoon clattered to the countertop and Adam's face appeared above mine, his brow furrowed with concern. "Lori? What's wrong?"

"It's gone," I told him, as the memories flooded back. "My car, my luggage," I moaned, grief-stricken, "and *Reginald*."

"Dear Lord . . ." Adam knelt beside me, put a firm hand on my shoulder, and said calmly, "Was someone else in the car with you?"

"No," I said. "Reginald's not a person. He's a"—I blushed crimson—"a rabbit, a pink flannel rabbit. I know it sounds childish, but I've had him ever since I was a baby. He's . . . he's . . ."

"An old friend?" Adam suggested.

"That's right," I said gratefully. "I have to find him. And I have to call my husband. He'll be worried sick about me." I tried to push the blankets aside, but Adam gently pinned me to the pillows.

"Lie still," he ordered. "I'll get word to your husband as soon as I can. I'd go now, only I don't fancy my chances, cycling to the village phone box on a dark road in a force-nine gale. I fancy yours even less."

A flurry of raindrops pelted the windowpanes and I flinched.

"Relax," Adam soothed. "You're safe. The hut's been here for more than a hundred years. It's stood worse storms than this."

I looked past him, noted the depth of the windowsills, the thickness of the walls, and was comforted. The hut was as snug as a cave.

"Where are we?" I asked.

Adam sat back on his heels. "We're in a fishing hut on the banks of a small stream not an hour's drive from Newcastle. We're a half-mile from the village of Blackhope and within shouting distance of Wyrdhurst Hall."

"You're kidding," I said.

"I'm not. If you'd walked a bit farther, you'd've bumped into the gates." The teakettle's low whistle climbed to a shriek and Adam stood, announcing, "Dinner will be served in five minutes, Mrs. Shepherd."

"It's Ms. Shepherd," I corrected. "But I prefer Lori."

"Then you must call me Adam." He drew me into a sitting position, propped the pillows behind me, and returned to prepare the teapot. "Are you a friend of the family?" he asked, over his shoulder.

"The Hollanders?" My stomach voiced its approval as simmering broth's savory aroma wafted my way. "I've never even met them. Mrs. Hollander's uncle hired me to do a rough survey of the books in her library."

"She's a Byrd by birth, isn't she?" Adam asked.

"That's right," I said. "Her uncle's Dickie Byrd, the industrialist."

"Then at least one of the rumors is true." Adam took a stoneware bowl from the cupboard. "The only one, I'll wager."

"Rumors?" My ears pricked up. "What rumors?"

Adam shrugged dismissively. "The usual nonsense. You know how country people are about newcomers."

As an American living in a small English village, I knew exactly how country people were about newcomers. If the villagers in Blackhope were like my neighbors in Finch, Nicole and Jared Hollander would be subject to all manner of speculation.

"Are you a local?" I asked.

"I'm a writer," Adam replied, not quite answering the question. "I rented the fishing hut to serve as my sanctuary while I'm finishing up my latest book."

"No telephone." I glanced at the portable typewriter. "And you don't use a computer, so you can't get E-mail."

Adam twirled his spoon in the air. "I'm beyond the reach of editor, agent, and publicist. It's pure bliss."

He strode over to a bookcase and removed an oversized, slender volume. I thought it was one of his works and expected him to show it to me. Instead, he carried it to the pine table, where he covered it with a thin white tea towel.

"I haven't a tray," he explained, arranging dishes on the towel-draped book, "so Ladlighter's *Illustrated History of the Ypres Salient* will have to do."

"Ypres," I repeated, trying to wrap my tongue around the awkward syllable. "That's from the First World War, isn't it?"

"Full marks, Lori." Adam looked impressed. "It's a town in southwest Belgium. The soldiers called it Wipers, and yes, it played a significant role in the Great European War. A quarter of a million men died there."

"Do you write about the, uh, Great European War?" I asked.

"I write about its repercussions." He carried the makeshift tray to the bed, and placed it on my lap. "Dinner is served, madam."

The bowl of rich brown broth had been augmented by a mug of sweet, milky tea and a thick slice of buttered brown bread. My hands were so trembly that I could barely lift the mug to my lips, and after watching me spill a spoonful of soup down the front of his sweatshirt, Adam took up the task and fed me like a baby. By the time he'd spooned up the last drop, my hands had steadied and I was able to finish the tea on my own.

I rested against the pillows while Adam rinsed the dishes, extinguished the oil lamp, and donned a heavy, cobalt-blue ribbed sweater. The sweater came as something of a relief to me. Adam Chase wasn't a big man, but he had an athlete's

build, and the rosy glow of firelight on his sculpted abdomi-
nals had been more than a bit distracting.

After adding a few lumps of coal to the fire, he swung the
leather armchair around to face me. "I suggest you get some
sleep," he said, easing himself into the chair.

"Don't you want to know what happened?" I asked.

"I can wait until morning, but if you can't . . ."

"The road was washed out," I interrupted. "One minute I
was driving straight up the side of a mountain and the next I
was hanging over the edge of . . . nothing. I jumped out of
the car just before it took a swan dive into the fog." I heaved
a remorseful sigh. The canary-yellow Range Rover had been
a Christmas gift from Bill, and now I'd gone and dumped it
in some godforsaken ravine. Along with Reginald.

"Do you remember what road you were on?" Adam
asked.

"I'm not sure it was a road," I replied. "It was unpaved,
about two inches wide, and nearly vertical."

Adam pursed his lips. "You must've turned onto one of
the military tracks. It doesn't happen often. They're quite
good about gating them. Didn't you see the warning signs?"

"I couldn't even see the side of the road," I told him. "Are
we on an army base?"

"More of a target range," Adam answered. "The army
uses the high moors for artillery practice."

"Well," I said, with a crooked grin, "that'll make it easier
for my husband, when he calls out the army to find me."

Adam leaned his head against the back of the chair. "He
won't have any trouble finding Wyrdhurst."

"What's it like?" I asked.

"Imposing," he said, after a judicious pause. "It's haunted, of course."

I laughed outright. "Ghoulies and ghosties and long-leggety beasties?"

"And things that go bump in the night." Adam winced. "Appalling, isn't it, in this day and age? But I have it on good authority that the ghost of Josiah Byrd walks Wyrdhurst's corridors by night."

"Whose good authority?" I challenged.

"My mechanic's," Adam said gravely, though his eyes were dancing. "Mr. Garnett is quite an expert on the man who built Wyrdhurst. Apparently, old Josiah was something of a terror. Still is, according to Mr. Garnett."

"If Josiah Byrd built Wyrdhurst Hall, he must have died ages ago," I protested. "Don't tell me the villagers still live in fear of him."

"People here have long memories," said Adam. "They weren't pleased when the house was restored and reopened. I think they were rather hoping it would decay into dust."

"Ghosts don't frighten me." Firsthand experience had taught me that the undead were more helpful than hurtful, but I couldn't explain my curious relationship with Aunt Dimity to a man I hardly knew. He'd suspect a serious head injury or, worse, a touch of lunacy.

"They frighten Mrs. Hollander," said Adam. "Or so I've been told. The villagers think that's why she's not entirely happy in her new home."

"I'd blame the fog," I said firmly. "Would you want to spend the first months of your marriage in a place with such rotten weather?"

Adam was silent for a moment, his eyes fixed on the fire. Then he said softly, "If you're with the right person, I don't think the weather matters." He looked toward me. "Do you?"

The loose ringlets tumbling over his forehead gleamed like ebony in the fire's glow, and his eyes were as dark as night. I felt a warm flush rise from the soles of my feet to the tips of my ears and averted my gaze, but didn't reproach myself. It seemed hardly possible for a woman to awaken naked in a man's arms without feeling stirrings of some sort. Besides, I knew I'd never act upon those stirrings. I was deeply in love with my husband.

"How long will you stay at Wyrdhurst?" Adam asked.

"I'm not sure," I heard myself saying. "As long as it takes, I guess."

"I'll cycle there first thing in the morning. The Hollanders will come to fetch you, I'm sure. But now"—Adam pointed a finger at me—"you must sleep. We can talk again tomorrow. If you need anything in the night, I'll be right here." He put his feet up on the ottoman, slouched comfortably in the chair, and closed his eyes.

A spurt of rain splashed down the chimney and sizzled on the coals. I slid under the blankets and turned onto my side to watch the fire, wondering why I hadn't told Adam the truth. I knew exactly how long I would stay at Wyrdhurst Hall: one week. I'd no reason to stay longer, every reason to return home to my husband and sons.

Yet they seemed far away at this moment. And Adam was very close. I peeked over the blankets at the pale, heart-shaped face. "Adam?" I whispered.

"Yes?" came the patient reply.

"Thank you. You saved my life."

"You took ten years off of mine," he retorted, and turned his face to the shadows.

Smiling sheepishly, I curled into a ball and plunged into a deep, dreamless sleep.

It was still dark out, and still raining, when I felt a hand caress my forehead and heard a soft, now-familiar voice say, "Lori? Wake up. Your husband *has* called out the army."

CHAPTER

A gray wisp of morning light revealed a tall, rangily built young man standing just inside the peacock-blue front door. His close-cropped hair was as fair as cornsilk, his face beet-red from exertion. He was dressed in a camouflage-print field uniform and holding a black beret that seemed to be soaking wet. His boots and trouser legs were liberally daubed with mud, and a dripping olive-drab rain poncho hung over the beechwood chair.

"Lori Shepherd," Adam said, standing aside, "Captain Guy Manning."

Captain Manning stepped forward. "I've been sent to find you, Ms. Shepherd. Your husband became alarmed when you failed to arrive at your destination yesterday afternoon."

"He had good reason." Adam folded his arms across his

chest. "Ms. Shepherd's car was swept away by a landslide on one of your roads."

Captain Manning favored Adam with an expressionless stare. "I'm aware of the situation, sir. I discovered the landslide late last night."

"Then you must also be aware of the fact that one of your gates was left open," Adam said.

"The matter is under investigation, sir." Captain Manning's grave gray eyes focused on me. "Do you require medical attention, Ms. Shepherd?"

"No," I said, pushing myself into a sitting position. "But what about my husband? Is he at Wyrdhurst?"

"Your husband is awaiting news of you at your home in the Cotswolds, ma'am."

When the officer pulled a cell phone from his breast pocket and offered it to me, I all but snatched it from his hand and hastily dialed my own number. Bill answered halfway through the first ring.

"Lori, are you all right?"

The raw fear in his voice brought home how close I'd come to losing everything. I had to press a hand to my mouth, to keep from blubbing.

"I'm fine, Bill." I swallowed hard and made a snap decision: I'd tell my husband the whole truth as soon as we were together, but for now I'd tone it down. There was no point in worrying him long-distance. "My car . . . ran off the road, because of the fog, and I . . . lost my cell phone. I lost my way, too, so I . . . spent the night in a fishing hut. An officer, Captain Manning, just found me."

"Are you sure you're not hurt?" Bill demanded.

"I'm sure." I hesitated. "The Rover's sort of . . . totaled."

"Damn the Rover!" Bill cried. "It can be replaced. You can't. Do you want me to come up there?"

"There's no reason for you to come up here," I said flatly. "It was a silly little mishap. I'm far more embarrassed than hurt, and incredibly sorry for scaring you."

"Not your fault," said Bill. "I'm just glad you're okay. Here, I'll let you speak with Will and Rob."

I don't know what Adam and Captain Manning made of the babytalk that ensued. They stood at a discreet distance— from me and from each other—until I'd finished my conversation. Then they turned, in unison, and stared.

Adam raised an eyebrow, saying, "A silly little mishap?'

"Well, I can't tell my husband that my car went over a cliff, can I? He'd come chasing up here and march me off to the nearest hospital. Then he'd have a nervous breakdown." I folded my hands atop the blankets. "I'll tell him the truth when I get home, when he can see for himself that I'm fine."

Captain Manning retrieved his telephone. "If you'll excuse me," he said, "I'll report in."

While the captain made his report, Adam sat on the edge of the bed, facing me.

"I'd let a doctor decide whether you're fine or not," he advised. "Hypothermia's not to be taken lightly, nor is shock. There's a good man in Blackhope, old Dr. MacEwan. Will you ring him when you get to Wyrdhurst?" He touched my folded hands. "As a favor to me?"

"I will," I promised. "But I'd better get dressed first or I'll ruin Captain Manning's reputation."

I dressed behind a blanket Adam had strung across one corner of the room, quickly donning the clothes I'd worn the day before. I moved gingerly at first, anticipating a host of aches and pains, but apart from a windburned face and a decorative assortment of bruises, I seemed miraculously free of injury.

Adam had brushed the mud from my suede boots, but they were still uncomfortably stiff and distressingly filthy. When Captain Manning saw that I had no jacket, he removed his own and offered it to me. Since he had the poncho to protect him, I took the jacket gladly.

Then I turned to Adam. "Thanks again. I don't know what I would've done if—"

"You'd've walked to Wyrdhurst," he interrupted, "and you wouldn't have had to spend the night in a humble fishing hut." He tugged the jacket's hood up over my head. "Go on, now. And don't forget to ring Dr. MacEwan."

"I won't." I looked over at Captain Manning. "I'm ready when you are, Captain."

"After you, ma'am," he said, and I left Adam Chase's spartan sanctuary, wondering how I could repay a man who seemed to need so little.

Rain was still drizzling from the cloud-laden sky, but the fog had loosened its grip on the surrounding countryside. As I stepped through the blue door, I had my first glimpse of the scenery Stan had promised.

The fishing hut stood at the bottom of a steep valley carved by a rain-swollen, coffee-colored stream that ran swiftly alongside the paved road, its stony banks littered with storm debris. Above the rushing stream rose a vast, undulating wall of round-shouldered hills that folded one into another as far as the eye could see. The windswept, sheep-cropped landscape seemed as old as time. It bore little re-semblance to the Cotswolds' cozy patchwork of field and forest.

The sight of Captain Manning's olive-drab Range Rover set me back on my heels a bit.

"Is something wrong, ma'am?" he inquired.

"It's just the . . . the Rover. I guess it reminded me of my accident."

Captain Manning seemed to give the matter more con-sideration than it deserved. "Rather a different color," he ob-served sagely, snugging his beret over his blond hair. "Canary-yellow isn't standard army issue."

I glanced up in time to catch a smile so fleeting that I thought I'd imagined it. "How do you know what color my car is? Did my husband tell you?"

"I found your car, ma'am. Last night." The grave expres-sion was firmly back in place. "It had tumbled quite a dis-tance. I climbed down to it, to make sure you weren't inside. When I saw the door wrenched from its hinges, I thought you might have been thrown free."

"I jumped out, just before it fell."

"I deduced as much." Captain Manning clasped his hands behind his back and stood at ease, scanning the distant ridge-lines. "After I searched the hillside, I climbed back up to the track and found tufts of wool from your jumper clinging to the gorse. Once I'd found the wool, it was a simple matter to follow your trail to Chase's place." He paused briefly before adding, "You walked nearly five miles, ma'am. Not bad, con-sidering the weather."

I looked up at his sharply chiseled profile, too awestruck to take note of the compliment. "You searched the hillside, Captain Manning? At night? In the storm? *By yourself?*"

"My orders were to find you," he replied simply. "I'm afraid that your car will have to be left in situ while our investigation is in progress."

I didn't mind about the car, but I did express concern about my luggage and shoulder bag. I kept mum about Reginald. I wasn't up to explaining the plight of my pink flannel bunny to a British army officer.

The captain assured me that my things would be returned to me at Wyrdhurst once his investigation was complete, then strode forward to open the Rover's passenger door. "Shall we get in out of the rain, ma'am?"

"Please stop calling me 'ma'am,'" I said, as he gave me a hand up into the car. "It makes me feel a hundred years old. I'm Lori, okay?"

"As you wish, Lori." He paused before closing the door. "And since I'm not your commanding officer, why don't you try calling me Guy?" Again, the fleeting smile came and went almost before I had time to register it. It was as if he regarded emotional expression as an unwarranted breach of military discipline.

Guy tossed his poncho into the backseat and climbed into the Rover, then sat for a moment, his hands resting on the steering wheel. "I don't wish to alarm you, Lori, but I must inform you that your accident may not have been entirely . . . accidental."

"Huh?" I said.

"As Chase pointed out, a gate was left open. It's an extremely serious offense to leave a gate unlocked. I doubt that any of my men would have been so careless."

"You think someone left the gate open on purpose?" I peered at the captain uncertainly. "Who would do such a thing? And why?"

Guy's lips compressed into a thin line as he turned the key in the ignition. "As I told Chase, an investigation is under way."

As we pulled away from the fishing hut my imagination went into overdrive. Was some vindictive idiot trying to make the army look bad by staging an accident on military property? I drew the captain's jacket about me more closely. There were thousands of ways I didn't want to die. Near the top of the list was as an innocent victim of someone else's vendetta.

"We try our best to protect civilians, as you can see." Guy slowed to a crawl as we passed a large white sign posted by the side of the road. The sign's triangular warning symbol called attention to the message printed in large black capital letters on a yellow ground:

DANGER

MILITARY TARGET AREA

DO NOT TOUCH ANY MILITARY DEBRIS

IT MAY EXPLODE AND KILL YOU

"Subtle," I said, gulping, "but effective."

"We post signs at the entrances to all military roads," Guy explained, "expressly forbidding access to civilian vehicles."

"Good idea," I said, "if you could think of a way to make them fog-proof."

"That's why we have gates." The captain depressed the accelerator and pulled away from the sign. As he did so, he nodded toward the rushing stream that flowed beside the road. "Remarkably good fishing, if you're so inclined."

I welcomed the diversion. I'd come to Northumberland for books and scenery, not exploding debris and near-death experiences. "What's it called?" I asked. "The river, I mean."

"The Little Blackburn," Guy replied. "It's not a proper river, just a trickle that runs into the Coquet a few miles below here. The name means 'black stream' or 'black brook.' It's thought to derive from the color of the water."

"Which is dark because of the peaty turf the stream flows through higher up," I said. I'd run into the same phenomenon in Ireland.

"Those are the facts," said Guy. "Would you like to hear the legend?"

"Sure," I said, brightening.

"According to the locals, the Little Blackburn flows with the blood of a thousand Scotsmen slaughtered by the English on the high moors."

"How . . . colorful," I faltered.

"Northumberland isn't the Cotswolds, Lori," Guy said. "You're in border country now. Every inch of land has been fought over for centuries. The hills around us are drenched in blood."

I stared at him, appalled. "You and Adam should get jobs with the tourist board. The *Cotswolds* tourist board. I don't think you'd do much good for Northumberland." I tossed my head indignantly. "You with your blood-filled river, and Adam with his ghosts. If I didn't know better, I'd think the two of you were trying to scare me."

"I don't mean to put you off," Guy said, "only on guard. The people in Blackhope are friendlier than most, but they're not entirely happy with the changes that have taken place at Wyrdhurst Hall." He turned his head to look directly at me. "Bear that in mind while you're there, will you?"

"Why should I?" I asked. "Are you expecting trouble?"

"Not necessarily, but if you run into any, please ring me." He pulled a card from his shirt pocket and passed it to me. "The number of my mobile. Feel free to ring me anytime, day or night." He rebuttoned his shirt pocket before adding, "Chase told you about the ghost of Wyrdhurst Hall, did he?"

"The alleged ghost," I retorted.

"A skeptic? Good. I hope you feel the same way after you've spent a night there."

"Don't worry about me." I swung around on the seat to face him. "I'm a mother, Captain Manning. What terrors can a place like Wyrdhurst hold for a woman who's toilet-training a pair of teething toddlers?"

Guy brought the car to a halt. "See for yourself," he said.

I peered forward eagerly, then shrank back in dismay. Now that I'd finally reached Wyrdhurst's gates, I wasn't sure I wanted to go through them.

CHAPTER

4

The heavy black wrought-iron gates hung from a pair of lichen-clad stone pillars. Atop each moldering column stood a menacing bronze figure of a predatory bird, wings spread and talons reaching, as if poised to tear the throats out of unwelcome visitors. I yelped in alarm when one of the bronze birds moved.

"It's a security camera," Guy informed me. "Mr. Hollander doesn't like surprises."

Apparently we passed muster, because the gates slowly swung open.

"Electronic," murmured Guy. "Controlled from the house. Useful, when used consistently."

The stone walls stretching outward from the black wrought-iron gates were webbed with moss and brambles, and the drive ahead curved upward through a dense growth of dark firs and encroaching rhododendrons. The curving lane was matted with pine needles and leathery dead leaves, the air heavy with the scent of rot and damp. We drove in silence save for the patter of rain as it slithered and dripped through the shadowy canopy, silvered here and there by vagrant gleams of watery light.

The dank woods opened suddenly and there, looming imperiously at the edge of a vast plateau of wind-scoured moorland, was Wyrdhurst. I caught my breath and touched the captain's arm, willing him to stop.

"It's . . . it's a castle," I stammered. "No one told me it was a castle."

"It's a pseudo-castle," Guy corrected. "A Gothic Revival country house built by a man with more money than sense. I'm not fond of the place, myself. Do you like it?"

"I don't know . . ." It was too much to take in all at once.

The open ground surrounding the queer edifice was bramble-choked and thoroughly neglected, but the building was immaculate. A pair of ponderous round towers pierced with arrow slits and faced in rough gray stone framed a center block bristling with a fierce array of turrets, balconies, and battlements. Grim-faced gargoyles peered furtively from shadowed perches, downspouts ended in grotesquely yawning snouts, and the deepset leaded windows were as bleak as dead men's eyes.

"It's . . . striking," I said.

"Not intimidating?" said Guy.

Wyrdhurst scared me spitless, but I wasn't going to admit as much to Guy. I motioned for him to drive on.

The captain parked the Rover beneath the crenellated porte cochere and escorted me to the iron-banded front door, where he tugged the bellpull. The door was opened by a middle-aged woman in a black dress, who motioned for us to enter.

As I crossed the threshold, I was seized by a dizzy spell so acute that my knees buckled and I would have fallen if Guy hadn't been there to catch me. He bellowed something at the woman and she flew up the staircase while he steered me to a high-backed settle.

"Sh-should have eaten breakfast," I managed, as the dizziness subsided.

"You should be in hospital," Guy shot back.

"I hate hospitals." I took a steadying breath and sat up straight. "There. Crisis passed. Please don't mention it to the Hollanders. I hate being treated like an invalid."

"You may be injured," Guy pointed out.

"I'm just hungry," I insisted, and moved on to another topic. "Who was the woman who answered the door?"

"Mrs. Hatch," Guy replied, "the housekeeper. Her husband is the handyman cum butler."

I nodded absently, too amazed by my surroundings to pay strict attention to his words. The entrance hall was magnificently medieval.

The tessellated floor reflected gilded coats of arms set into the coved ceiling. Two burnished suits of armor guarded the mahogany staircase that swept upward to a balustraded landing. Stag's horns, ram's skulls, and a miscellany of mock-medieval weaponry hung from the paneled walls, and a row of square-backed Jacobean chairs sat to one side of a massive fireplace.

Three tapestry-draped doors led to rooms beyond

the hall. Light was provided by an extraordinary brass-and-stag's-horn chandelier, and an enormous bronze gong in a wooden frame stood beside the door opposite the hearth.

I'd scarcely had time to absorb half of the details when our hosts appeared, descending the staircase, looking every bit as eccentric as their home.

Jared Hollander was the very picture of a proper Victorian patriarch—plump, prosperous, and a good twenty years older than his new wife. He wore a voluminous vintage dressing gown in quilted black silk with a bloodred ascot knotted at his throat. His graying hair was slicked back with a powerfully perfumed pomade, and the waxed tips of his walrus mustache looked positively lethal.

Nicole Hollander was dressed all in white, her slight frame overwhelmed by a frilled and beribboned dressing gown. She had luminous dark eyes, and her raven hair, bound in a knot on the top of her head, was so thick and luxurious that it seemed too heavy for her slender neck to bear. She trailed after her husband, clutching a fringed shawl of embroidered silk around her narrow shoulders, and hovered, meek as a mouse, at his elbow while he did most of the talking.

"Damn the woman," Jared boomed, as he crossed the hall to greet us. "I instructed Mrs. Hatch to take you through to the drawing room." He bowed ceremoniously. "I do apologize, Mrs. Willis. A drafty entrance hall is hardly the place for you, after your ordeal."

I rose, shrugged off Guy's supporting arm, and explained that Willis was my husband's name. "My name's Lori

Shepherd, but please, call me Lori. And Mrs. Hatch didn't leave us here on purpose. I felt a little lightheaded—"

"Ms. Shepherd nearly fainted," Guy interrupted. "I hope you've contacted Dr. MacEwan."

"Thank you so much for your valuable advice, Captain," Jared said tartly, then turned to me. "I've rung the local quack. He'll be round later this morning."

"Thanks," I said, and silently forgave Guy his treachery. Jared Hollander seemed to have a fairly testy temperament. I didn't want Mrs. Hatch taking the blame for my dizzy spell.

"I'm sure you'll want to freshen up," Jared continued. "My wife and I would be delighted if you'd join us for breakfast."

"Sounds good to me," I said, with utter sincerity. It had been a long time since Adam's bowl of broth.

"Jared," Nicole said timidly, "shouldn't we . . . " Faint traces of pink stained her cheeks as she nodded shyly to Guy. "Shouldn't we thank the captain for his help?"

"I don't see why." Jared acknowledged Guy's presence with a cold stare. "It was his bungling that caused the mishap. It may interest you to know, sir, that Mrs. Willis's husband is a noted solicitor."

Guy ignored Jared's comment and spoke to me. "Lori, about the investigation—if I might have a word . . . ?"

"Certainly not." Jared interposed himself between Guy and me. "I won't have you badgering my guest so soon after her ordeal. If you must speak with her, you may make an appointment to do so later, when she's had time to recover her wits."

"How about this afternoon, Guy?" I slipped out of his

camouflage jacket, stepped around my host, and handed it over with an apologetic smile. "Say, three o'clock? My wits should be fully recovered by then."

"Please, come for tea," Nicole put in, as if to compensate for her husband's bad manners.

"Thank you, Mrs. Hollander," Guy said, his voice softening. "I shall."

As Nicole emerged from Jared's shadow, I saw that her eyes had a strained look about them, as if she hadn't been sleeping well. I also noted, with a flicker of interest, the way in which her gaze lingered on the captain's broad back as he let himself out of the iron-banded door.

"Officious cad," Jared muttered. "I hope your husband will take the army to task for its negligence, Mrs. Willis."

"How did you hear about the accident?" I inquired.

"The captain posted men here, as part of the search," Jared replied. "They passed his report on to me. As your host, I had a right to know what had happened to you."

My heart went out to the poor soldiers who'd caved in to Jared's pestering. Determined to show more backbone, I squared my shoulders and gave him my most intimidating stare. "I haven't told my husband about the accident, Mr. Hollander, and I'd appreciate it if you'd leave the explanations to me. I don't want him worried unnecessarily."

"Unnecessarily?" Jared began, but his wife put a restraining hand on his arm.

"Lori is our guest, dearest," she reminded him. "We must abide by her wishes."

"Of course," Jared said stiffly. He paused to take in my bedraggled state. "A bath," he pronounced. "A hot bath and a change of clothing before breakfast, I think. My wife should have something that will fit you, Mrs. Willis. You're both delicate."

His choice of words floored me. I was a fairly small woman, but I was also as strong as an ox—no mother of twins could afford to be otherwise—and as tough as nails, as my recent five-mile forced march had demonstrated. No one had ever described me as delicate.

But, then, no one had ever called me "Mrs. Willis" more than once. Jared evidently lived as he dressed, by the rules of another century. In his Victorian mind, all women took their husbands' names and were, by definition, delicate.

"Nicole, show Mrs. Willis to her room," Jared said. "I wish to have a word with Mrs. Hatch."

"Please, Lori, come with me." Nicole led the way up the mahogany staircase, pausing on the landing to gaze worriedly at her husband as he bustled through a door at the rear of the entrance hall. When the door closed behind him, she sighed. "I do hope Jared will go easy on Mrs. Hatch. He means well, but he's more forceful than he realizes, and if the Hatches desert us, I don't know what we'll do."

"It must be hard to keep staff in such a remote location," I said, stepping past my hostess.

"It's nearly impossible," Nicole admitted.

I'd taken the lead now, with Nicole a few steps behind. When we reached the second floor, I turned instinctively to the left, then came to a halt, feeling mildly confused.

"I seem to be getting ahead of myself," I said, with a sheepish grin. "Am I going the right way?"

Nicole assured me that I was. "Our bedrooms are in the

west wing, the guest rooms are in the east. We've put you in
the red room."

I was a bit surprised to hear that the Hollanders had separate bedrooms, but I held my peace. The newlyweds' sleeping arrangements were none of my business.

The corridor, with its lush crimson carpet and brightly
striped wallpaper, was pure Victorian. Hanging lamps with
frosted globes and faceted pendants illuminated the passage,
and a series of sentimental landscapes hung above occasional
tables littered with a wilderness of small, shiny ornaments.

"My husband collects Victoriana," Nicole informed me.
"That's why we wanted Wyrdhurst. We hope to turn it into
a showplace for his collection."

"It's big enough to be a museum," I commented.

"Ninety-seven rooms," Nicole confirmed. "My family has
let the place many times over the years, but no one's stayed
for long. As you said, it's a rather remote location, and the
upkeep of so many rooms can be a bit daunting."

"How do you manage?" I asked.

"A cleaning service comes up twice a month from Newcastle," Nicole explained.

I gave her a sidelong glance. In my experience, it was de
rigueur for a wealthy homeowner to contribute to the local
economy by hiring local help. Importing workers from as far
away as Newcastle was tantamount to snatching bread from
the villagers' tables.

"Weren't there enough local women to tackle the job?" I
inquired.

Nicole slowed her pace. "A few came, at first, but they
soon left. They seemed . . . uncomfortable, working here.

There's a silly rumor going about that the place is"—she hesitated—"haunted. But I believe that they left because Jared found their work unsatisfactory."

It struck me that Jared's disapproval might have sparked the rumor. If the women in Blackhope were as house-proud as the women in Finch, they wouldn't have taken kindly to his criticism. They might have decided to repay his nitpicking by rekindling hoary tales about the Wyrdhurst ghost. It was just the sort of prank my own neighbors would pull, if I were ever so foolish as to offend them.

"Do you believe that Wyrdhurst is haunted?" I asked.

"Certainly not," Nicole said, much too quickly. "Uncle Dickie says it's absolute nonsense."

"I'm sure he's right," I said.

"He's such a dear," Nicole went on, her face brightening. "He restored the fabric of the building, updated the wiring and the plumbing. He even furnished the lower rooms for us. The third story's still unfinished, but I seldom go up there." She shot a nervous glance at the ceiling, then pointed toward a door to our left.

"The bathroom," she informed me. "And the red room—"

"—is next door," I interrupted.

"How did you know?" she asked.

"Lucky guess," I replied. "If this were my house, I'd put my guests close to the bathroom."

"That's what Jared thought," said Nicole. "I hope you like the red room. He selected it for you."

She opened the next door to our left and stood back. I stepped past her, stopped dead on the threshold, and shuddered.

"Oh, Lori, you've taken a chill. Go sit by the fire while I

run your bath." Nicole draped her gorgeous shawl around my grubby shoulders and left me standing mutely in the doorway.

I was glad of her absence. I needed a private moment to come to terms with the red room's sheer awfulness.

CHAPTER

It looked like a funeral parlor. Every ponderous piece of furniture was made of time-blackened oak or covered in blood-red fabric, and everywhere I looked, dead animals stared back at me. A stuffed ferret frolicked on the mantelpiece, a monkey crouched rigidly atop the wardrobe, and a flock of silent songbirds perched coyly in a glass dome on the dressing table. Reginald, I knew, would be appalled.

The fire crackling in the tiled hearth only made matters worse. The monkey's shadow quivered ominously on the ceiling, the songbirds' eyes glittered pitifully, and the ferret's fur gleamed in a grotesque parody of good health. The furniture's carved figures seemed to writhe in the firelight, and the crimson damask bedcover glistened like a spreading pool of blood. I could easily picture a hollow-cheeked cadaver lying in state on the canopied four-poster. It was harder to imagine me lying there.

I forced myself to step into the room and stand before the fire. The heat was so oppressive, the room's decor so claustrophobic, that a wave of nausea rocked me and I sank, wobbly-kneed, onto the red velvet fainting couch.

"Your bath is running." Nicole bustled into the room and opened the wardrobe. "I've put some of my things in here for you—normal things, not vintage clothing. I wouldn't dream of imposing Jared's taste on you."

"Thanks." I put a hand to my damp forehead. "Ruffles don't really suit me. It's like spraying whipped cream on a horse."

"Nonsense," Nicole exclaimed. "You've a lovely figure." She gazed at me expectantly. "Do you like your room?"

Nothing warms a mother's heart more than being told she has a lovely figure. I carefully swallowed the absolute truth and replied with a close approximation. "It's stunning. Were the stuffed animals always in it?"

"No," Nicole said. "Jared brought them up from the study as a finishing touch. We think the room must have been used as a nursery at one time. It's the only way we can explain the bars." She crossed to the windows and pulled the heavy drapes aside, revealing a row of stout iron bars set four inches apart in the stone sill.

The barred windows and the lifeless animals suggested a zoo, but the words that came to my mind were: *a prison*. I must have spoken the words aloud, because Nicole shook her head.

"The dungeons are down below," she told me. "Jared plans to use them as an annex to the wine cellar, once we clear them of rubbish."

"You have dungeons?" I said weakly.

"What would a castle be without a dungeon? My great-grandfather, Josiah Byrd, built Wyrdhurst, and he didn't believe in half-measures." Nicole peered past the bars. "We would have had a drawbridge and a moat if the workers hadn't gone away to the war."

A haze rose before my eyes. Despite the heat, my teeth began to chatter. I was about to ask Nicole to call for Dr. MacEwan when a pair of black button eyes twinkled at me from the bedside table.

"Teddy," I whispered.

Nicole followed my gaze. "His name's Major Ted," she told me. "He's been in the family for donkey's years. Uncle Dickie gave him to me when I was very small. I thought you might enjoy his company."

Major Ted was a toffee-colored bear costumed in the khaki field uniform and stiff, high-peaked hat of a British army officer. The jodhpurs, puttees, and flared tunic with its brass buttons were vintage World War I, as were the monocle and the brown leather strap running slantwise from shoulder to belt. The monocle was held in place—rather brutally, in my opinion—with a pin.

Nicole looked at me uncertainly. "Jared thought it a bit childish, but I—"

"It's not childish," I said. "Teddy's wonderful."

"Major Ted," Nicole corrected gently. She still looked concerned. "You don't seem at all well, Lori."

"I just need to get out of this room," I muttered, "and into a hot bath," I added hastily, when I saw Nicole flinch. "I'm really looking forward to a good soak."

"You know where to find it." The young woman gestured

toward a telephone on the dressing table. "Ring zero-five when you're ready. Mrs. Hatch will show you the way to the dining room."

I nodded silently, unwilling to tear my gaze from Major Ted's. Teddy was the only hint of normalcy in the room, and when Nicole had gone, I walked unsteadily to the bedside table and clasped the uniformed bear in my arms.

"You're not Reginald," I murmured, removing the offending monocle. "But you'll do."

The bath, the clean clothes, and Teddy's comforting presence made me feel almost human. A hearty breakfast far away from the horrible red room would, I firmly believed, finish the job. I pulled on the fawn slacks, nut-brown lambswool sweater, and soft leather slippers provided by my hostess and decided that I could do without Mrs. Hatch's services.

I didn't need anyone's help to find the dining room. All I had to do was follow my nose. The mouthwatering aroma of frying bacon drew me down the main staircase to the door beside the gong in the entrance hall. I was reaching for the knob when I heard Nicole's voice coming from inside the room. She sounded upset.

"Oh, Jared, must you go? You know how I hate staying on here without you."

"You won't be alone this time." Jared's bass rumble came through clearly to the entrance hall. "Mrs. Willis will be here to keep you company."

"But will she stay the whole week?" Nicole fretted. "She seemed ill-at-ease in the red room. If she decides to cut her

visit short, I'm leaving. After what happened last time, I re-
fuse—"

"How often do I have to tell you that it was all in your
head, my dear? Old houses make noises. You must simply accustom yourself to them."

"But it wasn't just the noises, Jared. It was the—" Nicole
fell silent, and when she spoke again, her tone of voice had
changed. "Yes, Hatch, the kidneys are lovely. Would you
kindly bring fresh toast for our guest when she arrives?"

As I entered the room, a portly, middle-aged man in a
black suit was leaving through another door, a silver toast
rack in his hands.

"Mrs. Hatch's husband," Nicole informed me, when he'd
gone. "They're both from Newcastle. We tried a local couple, but—"

"There's no need to bore our guest with tedious
domestic affairs, my dear." Jared rose to pull a button-
backed velvet chair out for me. "Won't you sit down, Mrs.
Willis?"

I sat opposite Nicole, with Jared taking pride of place at
the head of a polished walnut table long enough to seat
twelve. Behind me, a mirrored breakfront held an array of
covered warming dishes. While Nicole poured tea for me,
Jared crossed to the breakfront and took up a plate.

"What may I get for you?" he asked. "Eggs, kidneys, bacon, tomatoes, kippers?"

"All of the above," I replied. Adam's broth was but a distant memory and my stomach felt as empty as a pauper's
pockets. "Sorry to keep you waiting."

"Not at all," said Jared. "We rarely breakfast before nine."
He placed the laden dish before me and resumed his seat.

Hatch returned briefly to present me with a rack of fresh toast and I helped myself to the marmalade.

The dining room was another Victorian time capsule, richly papered, splendidly carpeted, and overburdened with objets d'art. My hosts, however, had made a concession to modern times by exchanging vintage for contemporary clothing.

Jared was all business in a natty black three-piece suit with a crisp white shirt and a silk tie. Nicole was more casually attired, in a flowing black wool skirt, an oversized black sweater, and woolly tights.

I attacked my plate in silence, aware of the tension in the room, but too ravenous to care. It wasn't until I'd quelled the worst of my hunger pangs that I decided to risk conversation.

"Nicole tells me that you collect Victoriana, Mr. Hollander," I said gamely. "It must have taken you years to find so many splendid pieces."

"Time is immaterial when one's passion is engaged." Jared twirled his mustache and surveyed the dining room with a benign, self-satisfied air.

"Most of the larger pieces were here when we arrived," Nicole pointed out. "Great-grandfather left virtually everything in place when he closed the hall. Uncle Dickie simply removed the dustcovers."

"My wife's uncle has been very helpful, in his way," Jared admitted, with a sour smile. "Though I dare say that my own collection has added polish to what was a somewhat mundane assortment of period furnishings. By the time I've finished," he added smugly, "people will pay to see Wyrdhurst."

"You won't have to pay, Lori." Nicole looked up from her plate with a bright, brittle smile. "But I'm afraid my husband won't be able to give you a tour. He's leaving in an hour. Going to be gone all week. Isn't it rotten of him, to abandon us while he goes off gallivanting in Newcastle?"

"It's hardly gallivanting." Jared scowled at his wife, then turned to me. "I'm needed in Newcastle, Mrs. Willis, to interview a new housekeeping service and attend several important auctions."

"We've been through three cleaning crews already," Nicole said, the smile tightening on her face. "Three crews in three months. It must be some sort of a record."

"It's too quiet up here for them," Jared commented.

"Don't they go down to the village?" I asked.

Nicole opened her mouth to reply, but Jared cut her off.

"Blackhope is an uncivilized backwater," he declared. "What amusements it provides cannot compare to those offered in Newcastle." He pulled a hefty gold hunter from his watch pocket and consulted it. "If you'll excuse me, I must throw a few things together before I leave." He leaned over to touch my wrist. "I do hope you'll forgive me for deserting you, Mrs. Willis."

I'd forgive him without a second thought, but I wasn't so sure his wife could. She watched with wide, anxious eyes as he left the room, and didn't touch her food after he'd gone.

I went back for seconds. "When I've finished breakfast," I said, piling on the smoked kippers, "would you show me the library?"

"The library?" Nicole's eyes took a moment to focus on me. "Of course. The library. That's why Uncle Dickie sent you."

As I watched my hostess slip back into a preoccupied silence, I began to suspect that the library wasn't the only reason Uncle Dickie had sent me.

CHAPTER

6

Dickie Byrd was a down-to-earth, no-nonsense kind of guy. It wasn't hard to imagine what he thought of his new nephew-in-law. Nicole might put up with Jared's high-handedness—love could be incredibly stupid as well as blind—but it wouldn't go down well with her adoring uncle.

Was Dickie worried about his niece? Had I been sent all the way to Northumberland to be a playmate for little Nicole?

Or was I an unwitting spy?

I turned the thought over in my mind as Nicole maintained her silence. The Serenissima prayer book was, as I'd told Stan Finderman, an awfully big payoff for a rough-and-ready library survey, but there might be more at stake here than the value of Wyrdhurst's books. Perhaps Uncle Dickie wanted an impartial observer to report back on the state of his niece's marriage.

I knew what I'd tell him, if asked. Bill frequently accused me of jumping to conclusions, but even he would have to agree that I was staring at an open-and-shut case: Nicole Byrd had married a pompous, pigheaded prig, and the sooner someone put him in his place, the better.

"Is it the kippers," Nicole asked, "or my husband?"

I looked up from my neglected plate. "Sorry?"

"To judge by the stormy look on your face, you've either swallowed a bone or choked on my husband's bad manners." Nicole had regained her composure. She sat with her chin in her hands, smiling wistfully. "Jared rubs people the wrong way, sometimes, but you mustn't think ill of him. He can be terribly sweet."

Marriage counseling wasn't part of my job description, so I kept my thoughts about Jared to myself.

"I am replete," I announced, pushing my chair back from the table. "Will you take me to the library? I'd like to get started."

"Are you sure you're up to it?" Nicole asked.

"Absolutely," I replied, ignoring the slight headache that had begun to tap at the base of my skull. Nothing short of broken bones would induce me to spend the day cooped up in the red room.

We had to pass through the drawing room, the billiards room, and the study to reach the library. Each room was awash in bric-a-brac, rich fabrics, and period furniture. It was so much like a museum that I found myself unconsciously looking for explanatory labels.

Nicole proved to be a knowledgeable, if mildly depress-

ing, guide. She pointed out collections of jet mourning jewelry, samplers stitched with morbid sayings, and a black veil
allegedly worn by the grieving Queen Victoria at Balmoral.
When she paused in the study before a framed landscape
made entirely of human hair, I searched for a change of subject.

"Is the village really called Blackhope?" I asked, averting
my eyes from the weirdly intertwined tresses.

"It's not as hopeless as it sounds," Nicole said. "'Hope' is
a corruption of 'hop.' It means 'secluded valley.'"

"And 'black' comes from the blood of a thousand massa-
cred Scotsmen," I intoned.

Nicole's mouth fell open. "How perfectly awful. Wher-
ever did you hear that?"

"Captain Manning," I said, and relayed his gruesome version of the legend behind the Little Blackburn's name. When
I'd finished, Nicole shook her head.

"Great-grandfather wouldn't have built his country re-
treat here if he'd known the legend," she said. "Josiah thought
bathing in the Little Blackburn was good for his health. He
loved it here."

"Why did he leave?" I asked.

"There were any number of reasons," Nicole said. "For
one thing, the Great War brought a good deal of business to
the family firm. Josiah must have been too busy to tear himself away from Newcastle." She crossed the study and stood
before a pair of finely carved oak doors. "I should warn you,"
she said, "that the library's almost exactly as Josiah left it. Uncle Dickie asked us not to touch it until after you'd com-
pleted your survey."

She reached for the oversized door-handles and pulled

hard. The doors opened with a nerve-wrenching screech, and together we entered a dreamscape of dust and old leather. Gray sunlight filtered weakly through a rear wall of tall windows overlooking a flagstone terrace and a tangled, matted jungle of a garden. The sun reflected dimly from the massive, clouded mirror above the fireplace, igniting fragile, furtive gleams on gilded leather.

"Oh," I moaned, my headache vanishing, "how beautiful." I sat in a high-backed armchair and gazed upward at the shelves, at the filmy cobwebs on the fine morocco, at the ancient, wheeled steps that would allow me access to the remotest corners of this precious and abandoned paradise.

"Beautiful?" Nicole flapped her hand at the cloud of dust that had risen from my chair. "You sound like Uncle Dickie. He's never happier than when he's clambering about a filthy old bookshop. I'll have Mrs. Hatch turn the room out before you—"

"No," I said. "Please, it's not necessary, unless you don't want your clothes to get dirty."

"I was thinking of you, not the clothes," Nicole said.

"Then leave the room just as it is," I told her. "If you'll give me some cotton rags, I'll dust things as I go along. A flashlight, er, torch, would come in handy too, and I'll need—"

"I stocked Josiah's desk this morning," Nicole interjected, "after we heard about your car. You'll find pencils, pens, notebooks, everything I could think of." She looked past me at the wall opposite the fireplace. "There he is, the old devil."

The hairs on the back of my neck prickled, as if the old

devil had crept up behind me. I rose from the armchair and turned in the direction of Nicole's gaze.

The portrait hung in a recess above a sturdy rolltop desk at the far end of the room. The oil paint had darkened with age, but it hadn't been very bright to begin with. The patriarch's black frock coat seemed to merge with the murky landscape, giving an eerie prominence to his stiff white collar, wispy white hair, and lavish side-whiskers. The effect was unsettling, as if the old man's head hovered, disembodied, in darkness.

His craggy face was hard, unyielding, his mouth set in an uncompromising line beneath a haughty beak of a nose and a pair of hooded eyes. Here was a man who saw life in black and white, I thought, who knew for a fact that God was, like himself, a stern Victorian.

"Great-grandfather would have abhorred Captain Manning's legend," Nicole was saying. "He had a great admiration for the Scots. That's why the library faces north."

"He must be pleased to know that they have their own Parliament," I commented.

"I'm sure he is." Nicole led me to the long wall of windows and pointed past the ballustraded terrace to an imposing mound of ivy rising from the neglected garden. "Josiah's mausoleum faces north as well," she said. "Although he died in Newcastle, he chose to be buried here. Jared wants to cut back the ivy, but I'd just as soon leave it. It doesn't seem right to—" She broke off suddenly and turned away, a troubled expression on her face.

"Your great-grandfather's been gone a long time," I told her kindly. "You won't disturb him."

"That's what Jared says." Nicole drew a finger through the dust on a map table. "Would you mind awfully if I volunteered to help you?"

I'd hoped to have the library to myself, but sensed urgency behind the soft-spoken request, as if the young woman dreaded the long day stretching out before her.

"You're more than welcome," I said. "I'd enjoy your company."

"I'll be back directly, then, to light the fire." Nicole flicked the dust from her fingertip and took a last look at the mausoleum before leaving the room.

I pushed up my sleeves and got to work.

The library ran straight across the back of the house. It was a high-ceilinged, rectangular room, with the fireplace at one end, the rolltop desk at the other. Deepset Gothic arches framed the tall windows piercing the long north wall. A fine brass telescope occupied the center bay.

The floor was covered with a dozen Turkish carpets, their colors dulled by a half-century of dust. An assortment of tables, map cases, and reading chairs sat in islands about the room, and an unyielding leather sofa faced a pair of leather wing chairs across the hearth.

I stood for a moment beside the brass telescope, gazing past the ivy-colored mausoleum to the desolate sweep of moorland stretching northward. It seemed odd to me that a man who could have afforded the finest tomb in Newcastle had chosen instead to spend eternity in such chilly isolation. As I reached out to brush a cobweb from the stone sill a gust of wind rattled the window, the ivy fluttered like a thousand beckoning fingers, and I fell back a step, my flesh crawling.

I tried to draw the heavy drapes, but they hung, rotting,

on warped poles, so I lit the lamps instead, all the while chiding myself for being such a ninny. I'd get no work done if I kept jumping at shadows.

Josiah's cold gaze seemed to follow me as I approached the rolltop desk. His expression was so forbidding that I was tempted to turn the portrait to the wall. I doubted that Nicole would have approved, however—she seemed to have a soft spot for the old devil—so I kept my head down, grabbed a notebook and a pen, and dragged the wheeled steps as far away from the portrait as possible.

I started with the topmost shelf in the corner nearest the study doors, selecting books at random and making notes. As I worked my way along the shelves, I could feel Josiah watching me.

I was halfway through the first section of shelves when the study doors screeched and Nicole came through, carrying a flashlight, a cloth sack filled with rags, and a coal scuttle.

"The Hatches are scandalized," she announced. "I'm not supposed to do housework."

"Jared's orders?" I guessed, from my perch on the library steps.

"He's terribly old-fashioned," Nicole admitted, "but that's why I fell in love with him. He's not like anyone I've ever met, and he knows so much about so many things, not just Victoriana, but life as well . . ." As she chirruped on about her husband's manifold charms, she bustled about the room, lighting a fire, handing rags up to me, and winding the silver-and-ebony clock that sat upon the mantelpiece. "Now," she said, coming to a standstill at the foot of the wheeled steps, "what would you like me to do?"

I put her to work recording titles on the lower shelves

and settled back to my private exploration, soothed by the fire's companionable flicker and the steady ticking of the ebony clock. I was so absorbed in my work that I nearly dropped my pen when Nicole spoke.

"How long have you been married?" she asked, out of the blue.

"Five years," I replied, gripping the pen firmly. "How about you?"

"Three months." She made a mark in her notebook before asking, "Do you have children?"

"Two," I said. "Twin boys."

"Twins." Nicole beamed up at me. "How splendid."

I wondered how long it had been since she'd indulged in a simple round of girltalk. The women in the village weren't likely to come calling and Mrs. Hatch didn't seem very chatty. The poor kid was probably starved for female companionship. I wasn't comfortable with the idea of spying on Nicole, but I didn't mind lending her a sympathetic ear.

"Are you enjoying married life?" I asked, resting my notebook on my knees.

"It's wonderful." She lowered her gaze to her notebook before adding shyly, "Though I somehow expected it to be more . . . tactile."

"Tactile?" I repeated, hoping for clarification.

"Yes. Well. You know." Color suffused Nicole's face. "Jared says that a relationship should be allowed to ripen before it becomes, um . . ."

"Oh," I said, clarification having arrived. *"Tactile."* I could scarcely conceal my amazement. "You mean, you haven't . . . ?"

"Not once," she said softly.

Well, I thought, that would explain the strained look in her eyes.

"I'm sure he's right," Nicole added quickly. "It's important to be friends, to get to know one another properly before allowing intimacy to blossom."

I dwelt for a moment on my first three, extremely tactile months with Bill before realizing, with a queer twist of dismay, that the face I'd conjured wasn't Bill's, but Adam's.

"It's unconventional, of course," Nicole went on, "but Jared's never claimed to be conventional. Besides, he's had so much to do, what with furnishing Wyrdhurst and traveling to Newcastle. He's not a young man, you know. By the end of the day, he's exhausted."

I banished Adam's image from my mind and focused on the present conversation. "How often does your husband go to Newcastle?"

"Once a month," she answered. "When he's gone . . ." She gazed pensively toward the windows, then came to the foot of the wheeled steps, where she looked up at me with round, solemn eyes. She was about to speak when a nerve-jangling screech intervened.

Mrs. Hatch came through the study doors.

"Lunch," Nicole said. "And, Mrs. Hatch, would you please ask Hatch to do something about those doors?"

We had an informal meal of soup and sandwiches in the dining room. While we ate, Nicole told me that she was an orphan.

"I was an infant when my parents died and Uncle Dickie

became my legal guardian," she said. "Uncle Dickie's the only father I've ever known. I couldn't have asked for a better one."

I attempted to turn the conversation back to where we'd left it in the library, but Nicole no longer wished to discuss what happened when Jared went to Newcastle. I didn't mind. She was so lonely, so unhappy, and so very young that I knew she'd confide in me sooner or later.

After the meal, she excused herself from library duty, saying she had telephone calls to make. I returned to my perch on the steps and carried on alone.

Two hours later, I was exhausted, filthy, and thoroughly dispirited. Josiah Byrd's taste in reading matter had evidently tended toward the theological. The fine morocco bindings, so enticing from a distance, concealed contents that were as dry as dust, and about as valuable. There simply wasn't much demand for collections of hellfire sermons and outdated Old Testament commentaries. If the rest of the books in the library proved to be as riveting as those shelved on the east wall, it would be a very long week indeed.

I was sitting on the bottom step, bemoaning the flagrant misuse of fine leather, when a gleam of color caught my eye, a sliver of orange beckoning like a rainbow in an arid desert. I got up to investigate.

At the far end of the bottom shelf, next to the rolltop desk, sat a slim clothbound volume that seemed to belong in another library entirely. I pulled it from the shelf and all but ran with it to the nearest lamp, delighted by my find.

"*Shuttleworth's Birds,*" I whispered, caressing the faded cover. The child's guide to common English birds wasn't terribly rare or valuable, but it was charming, filled with painstakingly accurate watercolors and lighthearted, whimsical verse. The title page identified it as a first edition, published in 1910, only four years before the author had been killed in the Great War—the Great European War, as Adam had called it.

I spied an inscription on the flyleaf, written in a youthful hand. It was dated October 31, 1910. Halloween, I mused, pleased by the coincidence: All Hallow's Eve was only six days away.

"To Claire on her twelfth birthday," I read aloud, "in fond remembrance of sunny mornings on the moors. Edward."

Lucky Claire and Edward, I thought, gazing out at the dreary garden. I'd have given a lot for a single sunny morning on the moors, and a friend to share it with.

I looked back at the inscription, wondering why I assumed that Edward was Claire's friend. He might have been a brother, a cousin, an uncle. Whoever he was, he'd taken pains with the inscription, centering it on the flyleaf, disciplining his sprawling scrawl. It seemed to me that *Claire* had been written with especial care.

Who was she? I wondered, closing the book. Nicole seemed well versed in her family's history. Would she know about a girl named Claire who'd been born on Halloween?

I started for the study doors, but before I'd taken half a step, a faint creak sent a shiver down my spine. Startled, I spun around, holding Claire's book before me like a shield, half expecting to do battle with Josiah's stern-faced ghost.

But there was no spectral figure hovering behind me. The creak had a wholly mundane source: a section of bookcase beside the rolltop desk had swung away from the wall, leaving a dark void in its place.

"A secret door," I said wryly. "I should have guessed."

Hidden doors and staircases were as common as fine china in grand houses like Wyrdhurst. Sometimes they were used by servants, sometimes by family members—I'd never run into one yet that was used by a ghost.

How long had it been, I wondered, since the door had last swung open? More interesting: where did it lead?

I gave the theological tomes a jaundiced glance, brushed the cobwebs from my hair, and decided to explore.

CHAPTER

7

The door opened on a hollow space cut into the stone wall. The air inside was frigid, the darkness almost palpable. I shivered, wrapped my arms around Claire's book, and switched on the flashlight Nicole had given me. Its narrow beam revealed a steep flight of stone stairs rising into the gloom.

"Hello?" I called. There was no echo. The thick walls seemed to absorb sound as well as light.

I strained my ears for a reply. When none came, I glanced half-longingly at the fire burning cheerfully at the far end of the room, and started up.

With every step, the air grew colder and the darkness deepened. The bitter chill lanced through my lungs and soon my heart was pounding hard, as if I'd run a mile. The effort made my head swim and I couldn't focus clearly. The walls seemed to close in on me, and a surge of panic gripped me when the hidden door creaked again, as if pushed by an unseen hand.

Then I heard another sound, a soft, deep-throated chuckle that seemed to come from nowhere and from everywhere. Claire's book slipped from my grasp and the flashlight juddered wildly as the evil, insane laughter filled the air. I turned, arms flailing, terrified, and saw hovering in the darkness, not ten inches from my face, a pair of glowing eyes, bright as young suns, that stared, unblinking, into mine. I cried out, stumbled backward in sheer horror, fell, and remembered nothing more.

"There's no sign of injury, Mrs. Hollander. She must have fainted. Exhaustion, no doubt. Her hands are like ice."

"I'll fetch another blanket."

"Wait. I think she's coming round."

Adam's face swam slowly into focus, his ebony curls backlit by dancing flames. When I opened my eyes, he murmured, "We really must stop meeting like this."

I managed a weak smile. "Where . . . ?"

"The sofa in the library," he said. "I didn't want to move you further until I was certain you weren't injured."

"We found you on the staircase in the wall." Nicole peered at me over Adam's shoulder. "The door closed after Mr. Chase brought you out, and we haven't been able to re-open it. How does it work?"

"I don't know," I said. "It just . . . opened."

Nicole eyed the secret door thoughtfully. "I had no idea it

was there. I don't think it's on the floor plans." She looked at me. "I didn't know where you'd gone, but Mr. Chase spotted the book you'd left to hold the door ajar."

I blinked, confused by Nicole's words, and Adam interceded on my behalf.

"Hot cocoa, please, Mrs. Hollander. And those extra blankets, if you will."

"Of course," she said, and hurried out of the room.

"Don't need blankets," I muttered, sitting up. "I'll be fine in a minute."

"That's what you said this morning," Adam reminded me. He moved aside so that I could swing my feet to the floor, and I got my first good look at him.

He was wearing a black fleece pullover over skintight cycling pants, and he seemed to be wet through. Raindrops sparkled like diamonds in his dark hair, his pullover had damp patches, and his pants and running shoes were streaked with mud.

"I should take you to task for overexerting yourself," he said sternly. "But you've had a hard enough lesson as it is. If you hadn't propped the door open—"

"I didn't prop the door open," I broke in. "I had a book with me, Adam, and I dropped it when I fainted, but I didn't use it as a doorstop."

"Then the book must have fallen where it did by accident." He pulled the cashmere blanket from my lap and wrapped it around my shoulders. "Fate certainly seems to be on your side. It's a miracle that you didn't crack your skull. Those stone steps weren't designed for soft landings." He narrowed his eyes. "I warned you not to overdo."

"I know," I conceded, "but overdoing seems to be my fatal flaw. Bill never tires of reminding me . . . " I winced as a sharp pain lanced through my head.

"Lori?" said Adam. "Are you all right?"

"I'm fine," I lied, and decided then and there to say nothing more about what had happened on the hidden staircase. If I started babbling about weird laughter and glowing eyes, Adam would whisk me off to the hospital to have my head examined. "Why are you here, anyway? And why are you so wet?"

Instead of answering directly, Adam reached over the arm of the sofa to retrieve a bicycle helmet from the end table nearest the fire. He cradled the sleek plastic dome against his chest, waggled his eyebrows, and raised his free hand with a flourish, asking, "Do you believe in magic?"

I laughed, taken by surprise. "Sure," I said.

"Abracadabra," he intoned, and pulled a rabbit from his helmet.

"Reginald!" I seized my pink flannel bunny and hugged him to me. "Oh, Adam, you *are* a magician. What on earth have you been up to?"

"You sounded so desolate when you mentioned the little fellow that I simply had to rescue him." Adam tossed his helmet aside. "Your cell phone was smashed to bits, I'm afraid, but your suitcase and shoulder bag should be in your room by now."

"How did you get them?" I eyed his bicycle helmet. "And how did you get them here?"

"I cycled to Mr. Garnett's garage to pick up my car, chucked the bike in the back, did a bit of reconnoitering,

spotted the Rover, and retrieved those items I thought you
might find useful."

His nonchalance was utterly disarming. I reached up to
brush the raindrops from his curls.

"Climbed up and down the mountain just like that, huh?"
I wagged a dampened finger at him. "Captain Manning won't
be pleased with you."

"So long as you are." Adam turned to stretch his hands
out to the fire.

"I can't tell you how grateful I am." While Adam's back
was turned, I subjected Reginald to a careful inspection and
found, to my great relief, that he'd escaped the wreck unscathed. "Oh, Reg," I murmured, "you just wait till you meet
Teddy."

Adam stiffened, his hands still reaching toward the
flames, but when he swung around to face me, he was smiling. "Teddy?" he said. "Do I have a rival?"

I grinned. "No, but Reginald might. Teddy's proper
name is Major Ted, and he's a very dashing, military sort of
teddy bear. I've nearly lost my heart to him."

"How did you meet?" Adam inquired.

"Nicole left him in my room to keep me company," I
replied. "He's right up your alley, Adam. His uniform is vintage World War I."

"I hope you'll introduce him to me." Adam leaned back
against the sofa's arm and favored me with a speculative gaze,
turning his head this way and that before reaching out to
wipe a dusty smudge from my chin. "Please forgive me for
saying so, Lori, but you look terrible. Why are you down
here, working, when you should be in bed?"

I grimaced. "Because I'd rather sleep in the fishing hut than in the room Josiah's given me. It's absolutely—"

"Josiah?" Adam interrupted. "Surely you mean Jared."

"Slip of the tongue," I said.

"Fatigue," Adam shot back. He got to his feet. "I prescribe an ample dose of bed rest, to be taken immediately. I really should be going anyway."

"Please don't go yet." Almost without thinking, I reached for his hand and gripped it tightly.

"No need to panic, Lori. I won't go if you don't want me to." He sandwiched my hand between both of his and sat again, much closer than before.

His gentle touch seemed to thaw the wintry chill I'd brought with me from the darkness on the hidden stairs. I lowered my eyes but didn't slip my hand from his.

"I've been feeling a little off-kilter all day," I confessed. "I guess the accident did shake me up a bit."

The study doors creaked open and Mrs. Hatch entered, with Nicole close behind. Mrs. Hatch carried a silver tray set with a cocoa pot and a pair of dainty, pansy-covered cups and saucers. She placed the tray on the coffee table while Nicole deposited an armload of cashmere blankets on a nearby chair.

"Should you be sitting up?" Nicole inquired worriedly. "I've rung Dr. MacEwan, but he's delivering Mrs. Martin's baby and won't be here for some time."

"Hot cocoa's all the medicine I need," I told her.

Nicole's gaze came to rest on my hand nestled snugly between Adam's. She quickly looked away, colored to her roots, and began to back out of the room. "I'll . . . I'll leave you to your visitor," she stammered. "Mr. Chase won't mind pouring, I'm sure." She gestured for Mrs. Hatch to join her and hastened from the room, closing the screeching doors firmly behind her.

Adam's eyebrows rose. "Have we started a new rumor, do you think?"

"I'd say we're good for at least a dozen," I assured him.

"She's very young," Adam observed.

"She's also married to an arrogant toad." While Adam poured the cocoa I told him about Jared's insufferable behavior, his disdain for Blackhope, and his refusal to employ villagers. When I accused the local ladies of resurrecting Josiah's ghost for their own vengeful purposes, Adam's gaze drifted to the oil portrait above the rolltop desk.

"If the ladies are using Josiah," he said, "they're doing a good job of it. When I told Mr. Garnett that I'd be stopping here today, he did everything he could to dissuade me. The man was terrified."

The evil laughter echoed in my mind, and for a moment I shared Mr. Garnett's fear. Then I told myself to get a grip. I'd been so jittery since the accident that I'd probably manufactured both the laughter and the weirdly glowing eyes. I reminded myself sternly that ghosts were a force for good. They didn't stick around on earth just to torment people.

"Mr. Garnett has the wrong idea about ghosts," I said.

"Perhaps," said Adam, but he sounded unconvinced. "I believe you were going to tell me about your room. I take it that it's not to your liking?"

"It's hideous," I declared. "Honestly, Adam, they've got me sleeping in Vlad the Impaler's boudoir."

"It can't be that bad," he said.

"It's worse," I insisted. "It's decorated with dead animals.

There's a monkey on the wardrobe who watches my every move."

"Why don't you request its removal?" Adam asked.

"I don't want to hurt Nicole's feelings," I replied. "The animals were Jared's idea and she worships the ground he walks on."

"Tell Nicole that her husband's furry friends wreak havoc on your allergies," Adam suggested. "Tell her that you'll come out in a rash if the creatures aren't herded from your room immediately."

I finished my cup of cocoa and sighed deeply, lost in admiration. "Why didn't I think of that?"

"Because you've been absorbed in your work," Adam replied. "How is it going, by the way? Discover any treasures?"

"One," I said. "It's not worth a lot of money, but it's my kind of gem. Where did you put the book you found wedged in the hidden doorway?"

Adam retrieved *Shuttleworth's Birds* from the rolltop desk and handed it to me.

I opened the book to the flyleaf as he resettled himself on the sofa, then passed it to him. "Isn't it splendid?" I said. "It's the best thing I've found all day."

Adam was so still that I thought for a moment he'd stopped breathing. Slowly, with the tip of his finger, he traced Claire's name, then Edward's. His hand lingered on the page, as he read and reread the inscription. Then he closed the book and gazed down at the cover, saying, "He was killed in action in 1914."

"I know." I called to mind the book's whimsical verse. "What a waste. Aubrey Shuttleworth was a charming writer.

His books are so . . . *civilized*. I've never been able to picture him in the trenches."

"He loved the moors," Adam said softly. "He spent his summers very near here. He knew every bird, every flower, every fish that swam in every hidden pool."

Sadness seemed to radiate from him in cool, dark waves. Instinctively, I put a hand on his arm, to comfort him. "It must be difficult to distance yourself from the soldiers you write about."

"Occupational hazard." He smiled briefly, but his eyes remained somber.

"Adam . . ." I hesitated, then plunged into my request before I could have second thoughts. "If you can spare an hour or two from your writing, would you consider showing me the moors?" I looked toward the windows. "If the fog ever lifts, that is."

"It will." Adam's dark eyes turned toward me. "And nothing would give me greater pleasure than to share a sunny morning with you." He placed the book on the end table and cleared his throat. "Have you any idea who Claire is?"

"Not a clue," I said. "I'm going to ask Nicole. She seems to know a lot about her family. I want to know about Edward too. He must have been a special friend, to give Claire such a lovely gift."

"Perhaps he was a little bit in love with her." Adam shifted his position, resting his arm on the back of the sofa to half encircle me. "I'm sorry your room's so grim and ghastly, Lori. I'd like nothing more than to bring you back to the fishing hut with me. But you really must stay on here, if only to find the rest of Claire's books."

"Do you think there may be more?" My voice sank to a

husky whisper and I trembled, not with cold, but with a sudden, intense longing that both baffled and distressed me. Before things could go further, the study doors burst open, the hinges screaming wildly in protest.

I had another visitor, and this one was livid.

CHAPTER

8

"What the hell are you playing at, Chase?" Guy Manning stormed into the room with a face like thunder, leaving Nicole to trail round-eyed in his wake.

Adam and I sprang apart like a pair of guilty teenagers.

"Ms. Shepherd's vehicle and the road leading to it are strictly off limits to civilians," Guy bellowed. "As you well know."

"Ms. Shepherd is entitled to her personal possessions," Adam observed calmly. "As *you* well know."

"Ms. Shepherd's possessions would have been returned to her in due course," Guy lectured. "In the meantime—"

"In the meantime," Adam broke in, standing, "she'd have been left without so much as a toothbrush while you dragged your feet with yet another of your pointless investigations."

Guy stiffened. "What do you mean?"

Adam eyed the soldier contemptuously. "I think you know what I mean, Captain Manning. I'm flattered by your interest, naturally, but if you have any more questions about my background I hope you'll direct them to me instead of interrogating my editor. If you had an ounce of courage, not to mention courtesy, you'd have done so in the first place."

Guy approached the sofa, his jaw muscles working. "I could arrest you for violating a secure area."

Adam stepped forward, until the two men were standing nearly toe to toe. "My editor would welcome an essay on military justice."

Guy clenched his fists, and Adam widened his stance, his thigh muscles bulging beneath his cycling pants. I was on the verge of throwing myself—or Reginald—between the two combatants when a gruff voice with an unmistakable Scottish burr sounded from the doorway.

"That'll do, gentlemen. Ms. Shepherd's had enough excitement for one day. You can take your discussion elsewhere."

The gray-haired man in the rumpled tweed suit had evidently overheard the argument. Now he strode purposefully into the room. He was older than Adam by at least thirty years and his head scarcely reached the captain's shoulder, but such was his air of authority that he made the two enraged men look like a pair of sulky schoolboys.

"You can apologize to Mrs. Hatch on your way out, Guy. She told me that you frightened her half to death, barging past her." He turned to Adam. "And you can wipe the smug gleam from your eye, laddie. It's men like Captain Guy Manning who make it safe for you to scribble your wee essays." He jerked his head toward the study. "If you can't settle your differences amicably, don't come running to me for stitches."

Adam retrieved his bicycle helmet before turning to shake Reginald's paw. "A pleasure to make your acquaintance, sir." Bending lower, he added in a voice only I could hear, "Until tomorrow." He straightened, tucked the helmet under his arm, and headed for the study.

"I invited Captain Manning to tea," Nicole was saying, in the small, helpless voice of a hostess whose plans have gone inexplicably awry.

"You'll sup with him on your own, then," said the gray-haired man.

Guy frowned. "I'd intended to discuss my investigation with Ms. Shepherd over tea."

"Ms. Shepherd is my patient, Captain, and I won't have her bothered," retorted the older man.

"Won't you come with me, Captain Manning?" Nicole pleaded.

"Thank you, Mrs. Hollander." Guy slid the black beret from his head, as if suddenly remembering his manners. "I'll call on you tomorrow, Ms. Shepherd."

"Perhaps you could come to lunch," Nicole offered.

Guy made no reply. He simply nodded to the older man, performed a crisp about-face, and marched past Nicole. It was only as Nicole was leaving that I noticed she'd exchanged her dusty work clothes for a flattering, midnight-blue velvet dress. I had little time to wonder if Captain Manning had noticed just how flattering the gown was, because the gray-haired man addressed me.

NANCY ATHERTON ⌒ 72

"I don't believe we've been introduced," he said. "I'm Dr. MacEwan. I'd've been here sooner, but I had a baby to deliver in Blackhope."

"No problem," I said.

"I hope the men didn't upset you," he said.

"Not at all," I replied. "Do you know what they were arguing about?"

"A military man and a military historian can always find a reason to squabble." Dr. MacEwan rubbed the end of his nose. "In this particular case, however, I can't blame Chase for being angry. I'd certainly take it amiss if Guy Manning looked into my private life. Though I dare say he's done so already."

"Why would he?" I asked.

"It's his job. He's head of security for the entire region. That's why your accident's preying on his mind. There's some might say it's his fault. It's certainly his responsibility."

As I slid the blanket from my shoulders, the doctor's bushy eyebrows drew down in a fierce scowl.

"Good God, woman, you're filthy. And what are you doing here? Exposure's no joke, young lady. Up to your room straightaway, and no arguments."

I put off my imprisonment in the red room as long as possible.

Mrs. Hatch had unpacked the luggage Adam had rescued from the wrecked Rover, so I grabbed my nightie and bathrobe and, with Dr. MacEwan's consent, retreated to the bathroom to dispose of the library's dust. When I returned to the red room after my bath, Dr. MacEwan had vanished.

I took advantage of the opportunity to call Bill. All was quiet on the home front, or as quiet as it could be with a pair of nineteen-month-olds ruling the roost. Bill was so exhausted by his first full day with the twins that he could barely string two words together, so I cut the conversation short, promising to call again the following morning.

No sooner had I hung up the phone than the doctor and Nicole arrived, the doctor toting his black bag, Nicole bearing a silver tray laden with a hearty meal. I looked from the rare slices of roast beef to the oozing blue-green wedge of Stilton, and felt myself grow pale.

"Perhaps a bit of broth would be more suitable," Nicole suggested hastily. When the doctor nodded, she departed, taking the hearty meal with her.

"Lost your appetite, have you?" said the doctor. "I'm not surprised. Sit up, now, and let's see what's what."

He took a stethoscope from his black bag and began his examination. He shook his head over my blood pressure, clucked his tongue at my pulse, and told me in no uncertain terms to stay put for the remainder of the evening.

Nicole returned shortly after I'd crawled beneath the covers. Dr. MacEwan took the tray she offered and dismissed her ruthlessly, ordering her not to disturb my rest. Then he stood over me, watching, as if to make sure that I'd eat up all my broth.

"Nicole tells me you fainted in the library," he said, when the bowl was empty. "It's a mercy you didn't break your neck. You've had a serious shock to your system, young lady. You should've gone to bed the moment you arrived here."

"I would have, except . . ." I looked pointedly from the ferret to the horrible, staring monkey.

The doctor followed my gaze. "I see. Not likely to inspire pleasant dreams, are they? I'll have a word with Mrs. Hollander."

"You could tell her I'm allergic to them," I offered.

"I'll tell her the damned room's gloomy enough without them." He glowered at the crimson hangings on the vast four-poster bed, then crossed to the windows to fling open the damask drapes. "That's better. A bit of fresh air is— Good God!" he exclaimed. "There're *bars* on the windows."

"I know," I said. "Nicole thinks it must have been a nursery at one time."

"A nursery?" The doctor snorted. "I doubt it. Tucked away upstairs, that's where you'll find a nursery. Not down here, where the kiddies' bawling might disturb the parents. Ah, well," he said, cracking a window, "the bars won't stop the breezes. Nothing better for you than fresh air." He returned to the bed, removed the tray, and placed it on the dressing table. "You'll dream about your accident, no doubt. Don't let it trouble you. Nightmares are par for the course in cases like yours."

"Once those critters are gone, I won't have nightmares," I assured him.

"Your confidence is admirable," he said dourly. "The fact of the matter is that you've pushed yourself too hard. You're bound to pay for it one way or another. Shock can affect the mind as well as the body."

I stared up at the bloodred canopy, turning his words over in my mind. "Could shock make me . . . hallucinate?" I asked. "Could it make me hear and see things that aren't really there?"

"What kinds of things?" he asked.

"Just before I fainted, I thought I heard"—I faltered, almost too embarrassed to admit the truth—"laughter. I thought I heard spooky laughter and saw a pair of creepy, glowing eyes."

Dr. MacEwan regarded me thoughtfully. "You've no doubt heard of the Wyrdhurst ghost."

I nodded.

"That would explain it," he said. "The power of suggestion working on an exhausted and therefore vulnerable mind can produce all manner of queer visions. Don't let it worry you. It'll pass." Dr. MacEwan hefted his bag and headed for the door. "I'll look in on you again tomorrow morning. Until then, get some rest."

When he'd gone, I faced the bedside table, where Reginald leaned companionably against the dashing Major Ted. Beside them stood a framed photograph Mrs. Hatch had taken from my luggage.

Bill's face grinned back at me, and I could almost hear the twins' throaty giggles as they wriggled in his arms, yet I gazed at them an odd sense of detachment. My boys were safe and happy, I told myself. They didn't need me fussing over them twenty-four hours a day.

Besides, I thought, rolling onto my back, I wasn't just a mother and a wife. I was a strong, intelligent woman of the world. Mr. Garnett the mechanic might be frightened of the house upon the hill, but I wasn't. As Dr. MacEwan had explained, my jitters were nothing more than an overblown reaction to stress. A good night's rest would put everything to rights.

Bolstered by my own pep talk, I saluted Major Ted, switched off the bedside lamp, and closed my eyes. Comforted by the dwindling fire's pleasant flicker, I soon fell asleep.

The fire was out when I woke up. I couldn't see a thing. But I could hear the stealthy footsteps and the quiet, raspy breathing.

Someone was in my room.

CHAPTER

9

My heart thumped hard enough to bruise my sternum. I took a quavering breath, gripped the bedclothes with both hands, and inquired of the darkness, "Who's there?"

A ghoulish, glowing face appeared above me, near the ceiling, a demon conjured from the Stygian gloom. Every hair on my body stood on end. I gasped once, twice, forgot I was a woman of the world, and screamed like a banshee.

At once, the bedroom lights came on and Nicole was by my side, apologizing, explaining, and beseeching me to stop having hysterics. It took a while for her words to penetrate. I was a little nervy.

When she finally coaxed me out from under the blankets, I saw, to my chagrin, that my demon was nothing more than Mr. Hatch perched atop a stepladder near the wardrobe.

He held the stuffed monkey under his arm and a hooded flashlight in his hand.

"It's only Hatch," soothed Nicole. "He came for Jared's pets. Dr. MacEwan told me of your allergies and I thought it best to move the animals at once."

"You were fast asleep when I come up, ma'am," Mr. Hatch chimed in. "I didn't like to waken you, so I come in quiet-like. Got the finches and the ferret with no trouble, but bashed the blasted monkey with my torch." He propped the creepy creature against the wardrobe. "You nearly knocked me off the ladder with your screeching."

"I'm sorry, Mr. Hatch." I pulled the covers to my chin, wondering why he'd waited until midnight to round up Jared's repellent pets. "What time is it?"

"Half seven," Nicole replied.

So much for the witching hour, I thought wryly. I'd been asleep for less than forty minutes.

Mr. Hatch clambered down the ladder, then carried it and the staring monkey out of the room. Nicole waited until he'd shut the door to speak.

"Please don't tell Dr. MacEwan that we disturbed you," she said. "He's already furious with me for letting you work so soon after your accident."

"It was my choice," I reminded her. "A foolish one, as it happens. I've been feeling out of whack all day. Dr. MacEwan says it's the aftereffects of shock."

"How dreadful," said Nicole.

"It hasn't been pleasant," I agreed. "My imagination's run amok. I've even started hearing things. I think they're called auditory halluci—"

"What did you hear?" Nicole broke in. She stood stock-still at the foot of the bed. She was wearing an exquisite slate-gray gown with embroidery and hand beadwork, and her dark hair fell in a wavy mane nearly to her waist. Silhouetted against the bedroom's rich wall coverings, she looked like a wild-haired damsel from a Pre-Raphaelite painting. "What did you hear?" she repeated.

Her insistent tone brought to mind the confession she'd begun but never finished in the library. I recalled, too, the conversation I'd overheard before entering the dining room for breakfast. When Jared was away, she'd said, she heard and saw things that disturbed her.

"Laughter," I replied. "I thought I heard a man laughing."

"Laughter?" Nicole seemed to relax. She came around the corner of the bed, trailing her fingers through the bed curtain's long fringe. "I've never heard anyone laugh. With me, it's mostly creaks and taps and thumps that sound like footsteps. The last time Jared was away, I thought I saw a face staring in at me through my bedroom window."

"Huh," I said, bemused. "I thought I saw a pair of glowing eyes."

"G-glowing eyes?" Nicole's seemed ready to pop from their sockets.

"Hyperventilation." I blurted the first thing that came to mind, in order to calm Nicole, but once the word was out, it made sense of what I'd seen. "Rapid, shallow breathing can cause a person to see stars, Nicole, and I was huffing pretty heavily on the staircase. The 'glowing eyes' were just the result of my brain overdosing on oxygen."

"Of course." Nicole seemed relieved. "And the only face

I saw at my bedroom window belonged to the man in the moon. As Jared pointed out, it was full that night."

"Still," I said, "it must have been pretty scary."

"I ran out of the hall in my nightdress," Nicole admitted, with a guilty giggle. "I was nearly to the trees before Hatch caught up with me. It took him half the night to persuade me to return to my room."

She slipped out of her shoes, and climbed up on the bed, leaned back against the carved post, and curled her legs beneath the full skirt of her beaded gown. She seemed intent on staying for a while.

I didn't object. If Dickie Byrd wanted me to babysit his niece, I'd do my best. Nicole brought out my most protective instincts. Apart from that, the adrenaline boost provided by Mr. Hatch's visit had left me wide awake.

Nicole twined a curling strand of hair around her finger. "A house like Wyrdhurst seems to encourage one's mind to play tricks on one."

"Especially if one believes it's haunted," I said pointedly.

"Captain Manning thinks the ghost is rubbish," she said, "a malicious rumor started by the charwomen Jared dismissed."

I felt a tweak of pride, knowing that the army's regional head of security and I had reached the same conclusion independently.

"It *is* rubbish," I stated firmly. "A big old place like Wyrdhurst is bound to creak, and I conjured the weird laughter out of thin air. It was probably nothing more sinister than a faulty furnace fan."

"It all seems so sensible when one discusses it with a

sympathetic friend," Nicole said. "It's quite different when one's alone."

"One's not alone, though, is one?" I said. "I'm here."

Nicole's grateful smile wavered as she looked toward the bedside table. "Is that your family in the photograph?"

I glanced at the framed photograph with the same sense of detachment I'd felt earlier, but this time my indifference jarred me. As if to compensate, I launched into a gushing maternal monologue that would have brought a strong man to his knees.

Nicole was made of sterner stuff. She willingly fetched more photos from my shoulder bag, oohed and aahed in all of the right places, and did not once allow her eyes to glaze with boredom as I yammered on about first steps and baby teeth. When I'd finally wound down, she returned the photos to my bag and sat once more at the foot of the bed.

"Your husband sounds almost too good to be true," she said.

"Bill's the best." I touched a finger to my temple as a dull throb announced the approach of another headache.

As I massaged my brow, Nicole fell into a pensive silence. I wondered if she was comparing my equal partnership with Bill to her oddly subservient role in her own marriage. I was searching for a tactful way to explain the difference between a wife and a doormat when the conversation took an unexpected turn.

"How well do you know Adam Chase?" she asked.

I shrugged nonchalantly, though I could feel heat rising in my face. It wasn't hard to guess what had inspired Nicole's inquiry. She was no doubt wondering why a happily married woman would allow her hand to be held so tenderly by a man who was not her husband. I had no ready answer, so I went on the offensive.

"I hardly know him at all," I said. "But I hope to get to know him better. He saved my life."

"Has it occurred to you," Nicole said slowly, "that he also might have put your life in danger?"

"Excuse me?" I said, hoping I'd misunderstood.

"You heard what he said to Captain Manning." Nicole twisted her fingers in her lap, as though abashed by her own boldness. "Why would the captain investigate Mr. Chase if he didn't think—"

"Are you telling me that Guy Manning suspects *Adam* of leaving the gate open?" I frowned angrily. "Is that what you two gossiped about over tea this afternoon?"

"N-no," Nicole stammered. "Captain Manning said nothing to me about Mr. Chase. I just thought—"

"I beg to differ." I leaned toward her. "If you'd *thought,* you'd have realized that Guy's job involves running background checks on all sorts of people. He's head of security, remember? He's probably got files on you and Jared."

Nicole smiled placatingly. "His file on me must be a tiny one. I can't think of a less rewarding subject."

My anger simmered for a moment longer, then went off the boil. Nicole was, as Adam had observed, very young. She had no idea how much trouble her absurd speculations could cause.

"I didn't mean to snap at you," I muttered. "The truth is, I've got a rotten headache."

"You're probably peckish. I'll have Mrs. Hatch bring something up." Nicole slid off of the bed, spoke briefly on the telephone, then returned to her perch. "Uncle Dickie's always headachy when he's hungry."

"Did you live with Uncle Dickie before your marriage?" I asked, glad to steer the talk away from Adam.

"Since my parents died, I've never lived anywhere else," she replied. "I was a sickly child, so boarding school was out of the question. I had tutors, of course, but virtually no contact with other children. When it came time to go to university, I simply couldn't face it. So I stayed at home with Uncle Dickie."

As I listened to her story, I began to understand what had drawn Jared to Nicole. Few women nowadays could afford to lead such a sheltered life, and even fewer chose to do so. Nicole's frailty and unworldliness would be irresistible to a man with such Victorian sensibilities.

"How did you meet your husband?" I asked.

Nicole motioned toward the bedside table. "Major Ted brought us together. Uncle Dickie asked me to have the major appraised by an antiques dealer in Newcastle. Jared was there, with an Edwardian rocking horse. I complimented him on his horse, he admired my teddy, and two weeks later we were engaged."

"A whirlwind courtship," I commented.

"Yes," she said. "Isn't it romantic?"

"Impetuous" was the word I would have chosen, but since my own courtship had been fairly nontraditional, I wasn't really qualified to judge.

"The engagement must have come as quite a shock to your uncle," I said.

"He wasn't happy about it," Nicole acknowledged. "He's always been overly protective of me. But I'd just come of age, so he couldn't stop me, and in the end, he behaved handsomely. Wyrdhurst means as much to my husband as Major Ted means to me."

She looked at the bear longingly, but I pretended not to notice. I didn't want her to reclaim my new companion until I'd had a chance to introduce him to Adam.

There was a tap at the door, and Nicole called for Mrs. Hatch to come in. The housekeeper entered, carrying an exquisite marquetry bed tray that held a pitcher, a matching pair of rose-patterned cups and saucers, and a footed pastry dish piled high with delicate, pale-brown cookies. She handed the bed tray to Nicole, added coals to the fire, and gathered up the tray bearing my empty soup bowl before leaving.

"Biscuits and a milky drink," said Nicole. "Uncle Dickie says it's just the thing to ease his aching head."

She placed the tray before me, propped on its little legs. While she filled the cups with a mixture of warm milk and honey, I reached for one of the cookies. It was a pretty thing, as dainty as a snowflake and faintly lustrous, as if each golden-brown whorl had been burnished.

"It looks like lace," I marveled, holding the delicate confection up to the light.

Nicole beamed. "That's how they got their name. The recipe's been in the family forever. We call them Claire's Lace."

"Claire's Lace?" The fragile cookie snapped between my fingers. "That's extraordinary. I found a book in the library this afternoon inscribed to a girl named Claire. I've been meaning to ask you about her."

"It must have belonged to Great-aunt Claire," Nicole

said. "She was Josiah's only daughter, the child of his old age. His sons were grown by the time she was born."

"Are there any more? Books of Claire's," I clarified, "not cookies."

"Possibly," said Nicole. "I believe I saw some books in the east tower."

"Those are hers," I said.

Nicole's eyebrows arched. "You seem very certain for someone who's yet not seen them."

I was certain, though I wasn't sure why. "Librarian's instinct," I said. "Josiah's books are in the library, so Claire's must be somewhere else. May I take a look at them?"

"I'll ask Hatch to bring them down tomorrow. If," she added sternly, "Dr. MacEwan declares you fit for duty."

The cookie was delicious—crisp and chewy and mouth-wateringly sweet. I washed down my first bite with a drink of warm milk, then asked Nicole to tell me more about her great-aunt.

"There's not much to tell." She sipped from her cup. "My great-aunt died young, in the influenza epidemic that killed so many after the Great War."

I sighed, touched by a faint ripple of sadness. Until Nicole had spoken, Claire had been a fairylike figure, roaming the sunny moors with Edward by her side. It was too soon to contemplate her death.

"It must have broken Josiah's heart to lose her." I felt a wisp of sympathy for the tight-lipped patriarch. "Maybe that's why he closed Wyrdhurst and buried himself in his work. Is Claire with him in the mausoleum?"

"I imagine so," said Nicole. "I suppose we'll find out once

we clear away the ivy. Jared has great plans for the garden. . . ."

Nicole moved from Claire's death to Jared's garden plans
without missing a beat, but my mind lagged behind. While
Nicole talked about herbaceous borders and flowering
shrubs, I envisioned young Claire curled on the library sofa,
laughing delightedly over Aubrey Shuttleworth's beguiling
rhymes.

When my yawns became ungovernable, Nicole moved
the marquetry tray to the dressing table, smoothed the bedclothes, and, at my request, closed the window Dr. MacEwan
had opened. Fresh air was one thing, I reasoned, but a room-
ful of dank fog was quite another.

Nicole lingered at the window, gazing past the bars into
the darkness beyond. "It's still raining," she said. She sighed
wanly. "You must think Northumberland has the dreariest
climate in the world."

Adam seemed to whisper in my ear. "If you're with the
right person," I said, smiling, "I don't think the weather matters."

"And if you're with the wrong person?" she said, so softly
and so sadly that I thought her close to tears. She picked up
the tray, turned off the lights, and left without another word.

I dreamt of the accident that night, but it wasn't the nightmare Dr. MacEwan had predicted.

The dream was brief but vivid. I was at the wheel of the
Rover when the road dissolved, but instead of tumbling
down the hillside, the car took flight, soaring over the moors
like a magic carpet.

Then Adam and I were together, inside a circle of stones that jutted like broken teeth from the tussocky ground. His palm was cupping the nape of my neck and I was pulling him closer.

"I'll come back to you," he whispered, and the last thing I remembered was the pressure of his hand as his mouth closed over mine.

CHAPTER

I foiled Dr. MacEwan's dire predictions by feeling great the next morning. By the time he stopped in to check up on me, I'd showered, dressed, and gone down to breakfast in the dining room with Nicole.

I was a bit surprised to pass a pair of burly men going up the main staircase as I was coming down. When I asked Nicole about them, she said they'd come up from the village to help Hatch bring Claire's books down from the east tower.

"Jared wouldn't approve," she said, buttering her toast with more force than was strictly necessary. "But there are some things Hatch simply can't do on his own."

Dr. MacEwan found me polishing off the last slice of blood pudding and marched me straight up to my room for a quick examination. He seemed almost put out by the rude vigor of my vital signs.

"I won't insist on you keeping to your bed," he grumbled, "but I don't want you to exert yourself unduly. You may be in fine fettle now, but chances are you'll be flat as a pancake by noon."

Nicole was adamant that I follow Dr. MacEwan's orders.

"There'll be no climbing up and down the rolling steps today," she declared, as we entered the library.

I looked pointedly at the tall shelves. "How would you suggest I do my job? Stilts?"

"I've made other arrangements," she said, with a pert nod. For someone who'd ended the evening close to tears, she seemed remarkably chipper. I assumed that nothing had gone bump in the night.

I also assumed that she would not be assisting me. She was much too nicely dressed to grub about in a filthy library. She wore a fawn skirt of the finest wool with an apricot-colored twinset, and her hair was arranged in a loose chignon that framed her face with spilling tendrils. She looked so pretty that I wished I'd taken more pains over my own attire. My workaday sweatshirt and jeans were practical but hardly fetching, and my sneakers couldn't hold a candle to the doe-skin shoes adorning Nicole's dainty feet.

"Come with me," she said, and led me to a sturdy wooden armchair facing the wall of windows across a rectangular oak table. On the table, between a pair of green-shaded reading lamps, lay an oversized gray ledger and a horn-handled magnifying glass. "Today," she informed me, "you can examine the catalogue."

"Stan never mentioned a catalogue," I said.

"Great-grandfather had it compiled," Nicole informed me. "It's handwritten, I'm afraid, but I'm sure you'll find lots of useful information in it."

The thought of deciphering handwritten descriptions of books I didn't even want to look at held little appeal. I caught sight of *Shuttleworth's Birds* on the end table where Adam had left it, and asked Nicole about the books in the east tower.

"Hatch will be down in a—" She cocked an ear toward the study doors. "Here he is now."

I turned to watch as the handyman trundled a coffin-sized packing crate into the room on a flatbed cart. The crate's lid had already been removed, and when Nicole directed Hatch to leave the unwieldy box next to my chair, I saw it once that it was packed tight with books.

"That's it," Hatch announced. "No other books up there."

I thanked him heartily and asked him to thank the two burly villagers as well.

"It really wasn't too much trouble," Nicole assured me, when the handyman had left. "Uncle Dickie's builders left a block and tackle on the roof, to aid in future repairs. The men from the village helped Hatch lower the crate to the ground, and he took it from there on the cart." She surveyed my work space with a satisfied air, then excused herself, saying that she had to help Mrs. Hatch in the kitchen.

Nicole's mention of kitchen duty puzzled me. She wasn't dressed for it, and from what she'd told me, Mrs. Hatch wouldn't welcome her assistance. Then I remembered the luncheon invitation she'd extended to Captain Manning, and all became clear.

I couldn't blame Nicole for looking forward to Guy's visit. What woman could resist a man in uniform, especially if the man was tall, blond, and handsome? Jared wasn't exactly love's young dream and he seemed to take his new wife for granted. If Nicole's thoughts occasionally strayed to the fair-haired captain, Jared had only himself to blame.

My own straying thoughts were another matter entirely, brought on, as they had been, by a combination of exhaustion and heartfelt gratitude. Adam wasn't just another pretty face. He'd saved my life, rescued my luggage, and—most important of all—restored Reginald to me. If anyone had earned the right to slip into my dreams, and an occasional waking thought, Adam had.

That settled, I pushed the handwritten catalogue aside and began emptying the wooden crate. The books it held weren't the children's books I'd expected, but they were interesting nonetheless: a selection of Sir Walter Scott's novels in pebbled red morocco; collections of Tennyson, Browning, and other Victorian poets; the complete works of Jane Austen, half-bound in dark green; and many more.

I knew in my heart that the books had once belonged to Claire. I didn't need bookplates or embossed stamps to tell me that they'd been her companions at Wyrdhurst Hall until a flesh-and-blood companion had come along to take their place. I scanned the flyleaf of each volume, hoping to find another sample of Edward's writing, but the endpapers proved to be disappointingly pristine.

I'd emptied half the crate by ten o'clock, when I paused to stretch my aching back, gazing glumly through the windows at the low-hanging clouds that filled the sky. The sunlight, even at midmorning, was weak and watery. There'd be no roaming the moors today, I thought, and my spirits plunged a little further.

A few crisp words from Jane Austen would, I knew, snap me out of my gloomy mood, so I reached for *Persuasion*. As I riffled the pages, a piece of paper slipped free and drifted like an autumn leaf to the carpeted floor.

I set the book aside and knelt to fish the loose sheet from under the oak table. The note was undated, but a jolt of recognition coursed through me when I saw the handwriting: it was the same sprawling scrawl I'd seen in *Shuttleworth's Birds*.

"'My darling Claire,'" I read aloud. "'The Ring at noon. Tell no one. Your own Edward.'"

I sank back on my heels, nearly swooning with the romance of it all. Adam had been right to urge me to stay on at Wyrdhurst and look for the rest of young Claire's books. The thrill of finding Edward's tantalizing note far outweighed the discomfort of sleeping behind bars.

Adam had been right about one other thing, too: Edward had been in love with Claire. Why else would he arrange a secret tryst at a place called the Ring?

I placed the note on the table and recommenced my search, but this time, I looked beyond the flyleaf in each volume. By the time the ebony clock chimed twelve, I'd found what I was looking for.

One hundred and twelve scrawled notes lay in a neat pile on the oak table. I'd discovered five loose sheets tucked into five different novels, as though left there by mistake. The rest had been cleverly cached in a hollowed-out volume of *Ivanhoe*.

The notes were brief, sometimes cryptic, but always written from Edward to Claire. Two-thirds of them referred to the Ring. It seemed to be the young couple's favorite meeting place.

One note suggested that they'd had an ally:

> *I leave in the morning. I'll try to come to you tonight.*
> *If I can't, look to Edith Ann, as we agreed. She'll carry*
> *my letters to you until I return.*

Edward's departure intrigued me. I hoped that he'd returned safely from his journey, and that Claire had received the letters he'd entrusted to the faithful Edith Ann.

I leaned back in my chair and looked over at Josiah's stern portrait, pondering his role in the romance. It didn't take much imagination to conclude that the old devil had disapproved of Edward. To avoid Josiah's wrath, the young couple had resorted to communicating through notes tucked into books and arranging secret meetings in a safe place, aided on occasion by a sympathetic confederate.

I wondered if the old devil had discovered the deception and brought an end to it, or if the affair had simply petered out, as so many young loves do. I wondered what had happened to Edward after Claire's untimely death.

Above all, I wondered how the two had met. Claire was the only daughter of a rich and powerful man. Her life had no doubt been severely circumscribed, her actions scrutinized, her guests screened.

Yet Edward had to have been a regular visitor to the hall, one with easy access to Claire's books. Had he been a distant cousin? A gardener? A tutor?

Or, I thought, my gaze wandering to the gray ledger, had

he been a lowly, underpaid librarian? I took up the handwritten catalogue, but before I could open it, the study doors announced Nicole's return.

She crossed the room with her head bowed, a forlorn slump to her shoulders, and handed a mobile phone to me.

"Captain Manning wishes to speak with you," she said, and flopped listlessly on a dusty armchair.

"Guy?" I said into the phone. "It's Lori. What's up?"

"Would you care to join me for lunch?" he asked.

"Aren't you coming here?" I said.

"There's been a change in plans," he replied. "I would prefer to dine in Blackhope."

"What about Nicole?" I asked. "I'm sure she'd like to come along."

There was a pause, the faintest of sighs, then: "I would prefer to keep our conversation confidential."

My interest was piqued. What could Guy say to me that he couldn't say in front of Nicole? I glanced at the catalogue, reminded myself that it would be there when I returned, and accepted Guy's invitation, arranging to meet him at the front entrance in forty-five minutes.

I folded the phone, returned it to Nicole, and apologized for spoiling her luncheon party.

"It doesn't matter." She sighed dolefully. "The captain has his job to do. I quite understand. Oh," she added, an afterthought dawning, "your new car has arrived."

"My what?" I said.

"Your new car," she repeated. "It arrived just before Captain Manning rang. I had the deliveryman park it under the porte cochere. It's the most extraordinary color."

"Canary-yellow." I rolled my eyes. "One of Bill's little jokes." My husband believed firmly that other drivers deserved fair warning when I was on the road. My latest misadventure had evidently done nothing to change his mind.

"The deliveryman left a packet on the front seat." Nicole stood and gave her dust-smudged skirt an apathetic swipe. "Would you like me to bring it to you?"

"I'll get it," I said. "It's probably a new cell phone. Bill thinks of everything." I placed the gray ledger atop Edward's notes and followed Nicole to the front door.

The canary-yellow Range Rover was identical to the one that had plummeted into the mist, right down to the heavy-duty straps installed to hold the twins' safety seats in place.

The keys were in the ignition and a brown-paper-wrapped parcel lay on the driver's seat. I opened the door to retrieve the parcel, but stopped short when an unfamiliar car emerged from the dank woods. The battered Ford Fiesta had once been solid blue but now was freckled with rust, and its engine sounded as if it had climbed one hill too many.

Nicole, standing at the top of the steps, peered over the Rover at the approaching wreck. "Who in the world—" she began, and her next words made my heart skip a beat. "Ah," she said, "it's Mr. Chase."

"I think I'll put my package in my room," I said. "I'll be right back."

Without further ado, I darted past my pretty hostess and ran up to my room to make the most of my own, more modest charms. I descended twenty minutes later, freshly scrubbed, combed, and clad in a nubby handknit sweater, slim wool trousers, and suede boots.

Adam stood in the entrance hall, chatting with Nicole. The light from the stag's-horn chandelier burnished his black hair with gold and warmed his pale skin. He wore the same black fleece pullover he'd worn yesterday, but the cycling pants had been replaced by a pair of black jeans. When his eyes met mine, my breath caught in my throat.

Nicole took her lower lip between her teeth, looking from Adam's face to mine with a worried frown. "I'll keep watch for Captain Manning," she said, and went outside, stealing backward glances as she went.

Adam took no notice. He brushed his knuckles along the side of my face, saying, "The roses are back in your cheeks. You must have had a good night's rest."

The roses turned a shade redder as my dream's final moments came back to me. "Once they took the dead animals away, I slept like a top."

Adam grinned, then cocked his head toward the front door. "I see that you've obtained transport."

"My husband sent it." The contrast between Adam's dilapidated wreck and my shiny new toy made me feel slightly ashamed of Bill's largesse. "He gave me the other Rover," I explained. "It was a Christmas present, meant to replace an old Morris Mini. My Mini was as beat-up as . . ." My words trailed off in tongue-tied confusion.

"Your Mini was as beat-up as my Fiesta," Adam finished the thought for me, adding, "and your husband is a very generous man."

"I'm not dependent on him," I protested, suddenly defensive. "I inherited a fair amount from an . . . an aunt."

Adam's mouth curled upward in a rueful smile as his gaze traversed the entrance hall. "Useful things, inheritances." He put a hand on my shoulder. "There's no need to apologize for being well off, Lori. We're friends, remember?"

His touch sent a surge of warmth flowing through me. The awkward moment passed and I looked up at him eagerly.

"You'll never believe what I've found," I said. "A whole pile of notes Edward wrote to Claire."

Adam's eyebrows shot up. "The same Edward who signed *Shuttleworth's Birds?*"

"The handwriting's identical," I confirmed. "You were right about everything. Claire had tons of books and Edward was definitely in love with her. They used to meet secretly at a place called the Ring."

"The Devil's Ring," said Adam. "I know it well."

"Will you take me there tomorrow?" I asked.

"I can take you there now," he offered.

"I can't go now," I said, with a pang of regret, and told him of my lunch date with Guy.

Adam's face darkened angrily at the news. "If that man tries to pump you for information about me, I'll—

"I can take care of myself," I reminded him. I softened the words with a quizzical smile. "Do you really think anyone can get anything from me that I don't want to give?"

Adam paused long enough to give my words a meaning I hadn't consciously intended. I lowered my gaze, but felt no desire to rephrase the question.

"I think," he said finally, "that I'm looking forward to our outing."

A delicious dizziness descended over me, and the room seemed to blur at the edges. Almost without thinking, I stepped closer to Adam, felt myself leaning toward him, but stopped when Nicole spoke.

"You'll want your jacket, won't you, Lori?" She stood in the doorway, regarding me anxiously. "Captain Manning should be here in a moment."

"My cue to exit," Adam murmured. He turned to leave and I walked out with him. "I'll come for you around ten. Wear your sturdiest boots and have rain gear handy. The sun may deign to show his face, but rain's never far away in Northumberland."

I waited until he'd driven out of sight, then, as if emerging from a dream, made my way slowly to my room to fetch my jacket. The brown-paper-wrapped parcel lay where I'd left it, in the center of the bloodred bedspread, but I was too preoccupied to attend to it. Instead, I crossed to the windows, to gaze across the open moors.

What had come over me, down there in the entrance hall? I was far from immune to Adam's charms, but I was also mature enough to resist them. Why, then, had I behaved like a giddy teenager?

I could no longer blame exhaustion or point a finger at heartfelt gratitude, but it wasn't simple lust at work, either. My feelings were more complex than that. One minute I wanted to mother Adam, to soothe away the sadness in his eyes, and the next I wanted to smother him with not-so-motherly kisses. I hadn't been at the mercy of so many contradictory emotions since the hormonal tidal wave of pregnancy had broken over me, and I knew for a fact that I couldn't use *that* as an excuse.

It was as if Adam had cast a spell over me. Because even now, removed from his presence and in full possession of my faculties, I could scarcely contain my eagerness to see him again, alone, at the Devil's Ring.

CHAPTER

11

Guy Manning arrived ten minutes later. Nicole sent Mrs. Hatch to fetch me while she lingered in the entrance hall with the captain. As I came down the stairs, I noted with some amusement that the library's dust had been thoroughly brushed from my hostess's fine wool skirt since I'd last seen her.

My amusement faded, however, when I remembered the quick-change act I'd performed upon Adam's arrival. If Nicole had a schoolgirl crush on Captain Manning, it was because she was, in essence, a schoolgirl. I had no such excuse.

I hated to interrupt what must have been the high point of her day, but Guy seemed relieved to see me. He nodded stiffly to Nicole and hastened to his Rover before she'd finished saying good-bye.

"What's the rush?" I asked, climbing into the passenger's

seat. "We're only going to Blackhope. Would it've killed you to spend a few more minutes with Nicole?"

"It might have." Guy's grip on the steering wheel tightened.

I glanced at him sharply, then turned my head away, abashed by my own clumsiness. I'd been so diverted by Nicole's crush that I'd given no thought to Guy's feelings.

"I'm sorry, Guy. I didn't realize—"

"There's nothing to realize."

"Right," I said, but he wasn't fooling me. The raw pain in his eyes had betrayed the pain in his heart. Guy Manning was in love with a woman who was, by virtue of a slender band of gold, beyond his reach.

The fog had cleared from the top of the plateau, but the woods were alive with residual wisps that hovered like recumbent ghosts along the rain-blackened branches. The queer, sunless patch of forest seemed to exert a silencing spell over Guy and me. Neither of us spoke until we'd passed through the camera-capped gateposts and turned onto the main road.

"Mrs. Hollander is a tenderhearted, innocent young woman," Guy said calmly. "Any man with a scrap of decency would be concerned for her well-being."

I gave him a sidelong look. "Is there a reason to be concerned for well-being?"

"You must have noticed how ill-at-ease she is in her new home," Guy replied.

"She thinks it's haunted," I told him. "She thought she saw the ghost at her window, and she hears strange noises at night—footsteps, odd creaks. Jared's never there to hear them, so he thinks she's imagining things. If you ask me . . ." I paused as my mind caught a whiff of an idea.

I silently replayed Jared's casual announcement of his latest trip, and his callous reaction to Nicole's fears: *How often do I have to tell you that it was all in your head, my dear? Old houses make noises. You must simply accustom yourself to them.*

I recalled the weird laughter I'd heard in the hidden staircase, and the glowing eyes hovering in the dark, and began to feel angry.

"Guy," I said, "stop the car."

He pulled to the side of the road and switched off the engine.

"What does Jared Hollander do for a living?" I asked.

"A murky subject," Guy replied. "He seems to spend a great deal of time at antiques fairs and auction houses, acquiring furniture for Wyrdhurst Hall."

"Not what I'd call a lucrative profession," I observed.

"Nor I," Guy agreed. "Your point being . . . ?"

"I'm getting to it." I stared into the middle distance as the vague idea began to take on a recognizable shape. "What if Jared doesn't actually go to Newcastle? What if he pretends to leave, hides his car somewhere, and sneaks back into Wyrdhurst?" My voice sank to a murmur. "It was a man's voice I heard."

"Where?" said Guy, clearly bewildered. "When?"

"Yesterday," I told him. "I was on a hidden staircase in the library when—" I stopped short as another thought occurred to me. "Maybe he was waiting to ambush Nicole and got me instead."

"*Who* was waiting to ambush Nicole?" Guy demanded.

"Jared, of course." I turned to face him. "What if he's *trying* to frighten Nicole?"

"Why would he—" Guy fell silent for a moment before observing thoughtfully, "Mrs. Hollander is a very wealthy young woman."

"She's a wealthy young woman with a delicate constitution," I pointed out.

"And a lively imagination," Guy added.

I folded my arms. "So here we have a wealthy young woman with a delicate constitution and a lively imagination spending one week out of every month virtually alone in a supposedly haunted house—a house *her husband* insisted on acquiring."

"A house where strange things happen only when her husband is away." Guy's brow furrowed. "Interesting . . ."

We sat ruminating in silence while the rain pattered gently on the windshield. When we spoke again, our words collided and it took a moment to sort them out.

"You go first," Guy ordered.

"Okay." I took a deep breath. "What if *Jared* is masquerading as the Wyrdhurst ghost? What if he's manufacturing queer noises, appearing at her window in the dead of night, using the legend to terrorize her? What if he's trying to frighten Nicole intentionally?"

"It might be in his interest to do so," Guy conceded.

"It sure would," I agreed. "Because if he managed to drive Nicole nuts or"—I thought of my tumble down the stone stairs—"cause a fatal accident, God forbid, well, then . . ." I shrugged. "Jared would be a very wealthy man."

"He's a wealthy man already," Guy reminded me. "He and Nicole are married. What's hers is his."

"That depends on what you mean by married," I retorted. "They have separate bedrooms, Guy. I mean, the marriage hasn't even been—" I broke off, appalled by my indiscretion, but it was too late.

"It hasn't been *consummated?*" Guy exclaimed.

"I shouldn't have mentioned it." I ducked my head. "Nicole told me in confidence."

"It won't go any further," Guy promised. He looked stunned, as if he couldn't imagine a man wanting to share Nicole's life without sharing her bed.

"My point is," I went on, "that Jared isn't behaving the way a happy newlywed usually behaves. He leaves his wife alone way too often, and he doesn't give a hoot about her fears. In fact, he keeps telling her they're all in her head."

"And she's naïve enough to believe him." Guy sighed wistfully, but his jaw was set as he pulled the cell phone from his pocket. "Perhaps I will make a few inquiries. It might be instructive to learn whether or not Mr. Hollander has gone to Newcastle in the past three months."

I suspected that the captain would know the brand of Jared's socks by the time he was finished. And I knew for certain that, if Jared had hatched a scheme to gaslight his young wife, he'd live to regret it. If Dickie Byrd didn't hang him out to dry, I would.

The Little Blackburn curved away to our left as the main road became Blackhope's high street. The village was larger than I'd expected. The houses, shrouded with ivy and screened by shrubs, crept up the hillside to cluster safely above the swollen stream. The pinnacled church tower rose highest of all, overlooking the narrow valley from a lofty prominence. Near it stood a larger, castellated tower built of rough-hewn gray stone.

"What's that?" I asked, pointing to the tower.

"It's a fifteenth-century pele tower," Guy explained. "A fortified house, built to protect the villagers from Scottish raiders. You'll find a castle in every backyard in Northumberland. They're picturesque, but they weren't built for decorative purposes."

It seemed to me as though nothing in Blackhope had been built for decorative purposes. The houses had no color, apart from shades of gray. Black slate roofs slick with rain gleamed dully beneath leafless branches, and every window frame and door was a matching, dingy white.

I was a bit puzzled when Guy pulled into the graveled parking lot beside Her Majesty's, the local pub. The pub in Finch was where people went when they wanted to spread news as fast as possible—not the sort of place I'd choose for a private conversation.

But Her Majesty's wasn't the sort of place I'd have chosen for lunch, either. It was an unappealing two-story building clad in the ubiquitous gray stone. Even the pub sign lacked vibrancy. The primitive portrait of Queen Victoria in black gown and white lace headdress was as close to monochrome as made no difference.

"What an appropriate name," I commented, as we sloshed our way to the front door. "Queen Victoria would like it here. Blackhope looks as though it's in a state of perpetual mourning."

"What village looks its best in late October?" Guy

chided. "Come back in August, when the heather's on the hills. It'll take your breath away."

The pub's interior was as cheerless as its exterior. A dozen wooden tables with round-backed captain's chairs filled the space between the fireplace and the bar. A bank of video games bleeped annoyingly in one corner, a well-punctured dartboard hung on the well-punctured wall opposite, and the bar itself was Formica-topped, utilitarian, and not as clean as one might have hoped.

The air was blue with cigarette smoke and stank of stale beer. The only attempt at decoration was an arrangement of three framed photographs surmounted by a Union Jack on the wall behind the bar. The large color portrait of Queen Elizabeth II was flanked by slightly smaller portraits of Prince Charles and Prince William. There was no mistaking which side of the border Her Majesty's was on.

The pub's occupants, a dozen or so men, sat at the tables clustered near the fireplace. At one, a foursome was playing cards. I recognized two of the card players. I'd last seen them on the stairs at Wyrdhurst Hall, on their way up to the east tower to help Hatch retrieve Claire's books. Before I could mention the coincidence to Guy, the man behind the bar called a greeting to us.

He was a veritable giant, well over six feet tall, broad-shouldered, barrel-chested, blue-eyed, and blond as a Viking. A winning smile gleamed from beneath his shaggy blond mustache as he came over to welcome us.

"Captain Manning," he boomed. "An honor to see you, sir. Here for lunch, are you?" When Guy nodded, the man bellowed toward the back of the pub, "James! Customers!"

I nearly ducked behind Guy when the giant stuck a shovel-sized hand in my direction.

"And who would this lovely lady be, sir?" he asked.

Guy turned to me. "Bart Little, may I introduce Ms. Lori Shepherd? Bart owns Her Majesty's," he added. "James is his son."

"Ms. Shepherd, is it?" Bart Little's ice-blue eyes flickered over me from head to toe. "You're the lady who had the accident, aren't you? A near thing, that. It's good to see you looking so well, ma'am."

"Thanks," I said, shaking his hand.

"You all right up there in the big house?" he inquired solicitously. "All on your own, aren't you?"

"No," I said. "Mrs. Hollander's with me, and so are the Hatches."

"Still, it's off by itself, isn't it?" Bart cocked his head to one side. "No one'll hear if you call for help."

"Why should I need help?" I asked.

"Haven't you heard?" Bart seemed to grow even larger as he leaned toward me. "The place is crawling with ghosts."

I held my ground. "Ghosts don't bother me, Mr. Little."

Bart let loose a roar of laughter and planted his hands on his hips. "Ah, a plucky one. I love 'em when they're plucky, don't you, lads?"

The card players rumbled their assent and Bart motioned us toward a table near the rain-blurred front window.

"Have a seat," he said. "I'll see what's keeping James. Fiddling with his computer, no doubt. Gadget-mad, the lad is."

"Mr. *Little?*" I said under my breath, as Bart exited through a rear door.

"I'd refrain from ironical comment, if I were you." Guy helped me take off my jacket and pulled a chair out for me. "Bart's heard them all and no longer finds them amusing."

"He's got a sense of humor, though," I said, when we were both seated. "Couldn't resist yanking my chain about the Wyrdhurst ghost. Wait till he finds out—"

"Here's James," Guy interrupted, shooting me a warning look. Our suspicions about the ghost's true identity were evidently not open for discussion in the pub.

Bart Little emerged from a door at the rear of the pub accompanied by a somewhat nervous-looking teenaged version of himself. The husky young man colored to his roots when I said hello, and studiously avoided making eye contact with me. I wondered what mischief he'd been up to when his father had summoned him. To judge by his shame-faced expression, he'd been downloading naughty pictures from the Net.

James took our food order, and Bart served our drinks, a cider for me, a lager for Guy. When Guy reached for his wallet, Bart waved him off.

"You're willing to pay for my freedom with your life, sir. I wouldn't dream of charging you for a meal. And there's no need to signal for a fresh pint. I'll see that you're well supplied." He gave our table a quick wipe and returned to the bar, to keep an eagle eye on our drinks.

Guy sampled his lager before taking a pen and a black notebook from the breast pocket of his uniform shirt. "Now, Ms. Shepherd," he began, "about your accident . . ."

Guy's interrogation was as far from confidential as it could get. He even raised his voice at times, to be heard over the video games: When had the accident taken place? Had

I seen or heard anything out of the ordinary? Why hadn't I heeded the warning sign posted on the gate? I was about to inquire politely why I needed to repeat answers I'd already given him during our drive to Wyrdhurst when he startled me by asking:

"Do you have any known enemies in the area?"

I eyed him doubtfully. "I've never set foot in the area, Guy. How could I have enemies, known or unknown?"

"You've no idea why anyone might try to kill you?" he pressed.

"Did someone try to kill me?" I asked, vaguely alarmed.

"Whoever left the gate open is guilty of attempted murder," Guy said sternly, "and will be prosecuted to the full extent of the law. Cheers." He raised his glass and drank deeply, then returned the pen and notebook to his shirt pocket.

My steak-and-kidney pie looked tasty, but I might as well have been munching hay. I couldn't get Guy's final question out of my mind. He'd warned me from the start that someone might have left the gate open with malice aforethought, but he hadn't intimated that the malice might have been aimed at me personally.

Try as I might, I couldn't imagine why anyone would want to kill me, nor could I think of a more haphazard way of committing murder. I hadn't been carjacked or tricked into taking the military track. I'd turned onto it purely by chance. No one could have planned my crash in advance.

A thousand questions teemed on the tip of my tongue, but Guy forestalled them by asking after my work in the library. When I mentioned the two men who'd helped Hatch with Claire's books, he suggested that I thank them.

"They're Bart's brothers," he informed me. "Bert and Brett will appreciate a kind word from you."

As soon as the bashful James had cleared the table, we walked over to speak with Bart's brothers. The men hardly looked up from their cards. Indeed, Bert and Brett Little seemed to hunch lower in their chairs, as if embarrassed by my attentions.

"I just wanted to, uh, thank you for helping Mr. Hatch," I faltered. I was unaccustomed to addressing the tops of people's heads. "It was, um, really kind of you."

The Littles mumbled something incoherent and continued with their game.

"The lads're at your service, Ms. Shepherd," Bart called from behind the bar. "If you or Mrs. Hollander need a hand with anything else, ring me and I'll send 'em up to you."

"Will do," I called back. "Thanks for the lunch."

"Come by any time," said Bart. "Your money's no good here, either."

"Free lunch by association," I mused aloud, as we exited the pub. "I should hang out with soldiers more often."

"Bart's offer has nothing to do with me," Guy countered. "It's your pluck he admires."

"Plucky me," I muttered. I waited until we were halfway to the car before grasping Guy's elbow and stepping in front of him. "Okay, Captain, are you going to tell me what that song and dance was about or do I have to guess?"

"What song and dance?" said Guy.

I eyed him skeptically, then spoke in a stage whisper. "Everyone in the pub could hear us." I lifted my hands, palms upward. "You might as well have printed our conversation on a billboard. Did you want to be overheard? And do you honestly believe that someone was trying to kill me?"

Guy peered at the clearing sky, clasped his hands behind his back, and squared his shoulders. "It's stopped raining," he observed. "Shall we take a stroll, Lori? There's something I'd like to show you."

CHAPTER

12

The streets of Blackhope were deserted, but our passage did not go unnoticed. Curtains twitched as Guy led me up a rain-slicked lane, and pale, furtive faces peered out from ivy-clad windows. I was acutely conscious of the covert scrutiny, and it crossed my mind to wonder if there was any real point to our walk, or if Guy was merely parading me before the villagers, letting them get a good look at "the lady who had the accident."

We didn't stop until we reached the church. It stood above and slightly apart from the village, separated from the pele tower by a soggy churchyard. The view from the church-yard gate would have been spectacular if clouds hadn't obscured the horizon.

I paused at the church gate to catch my breath before following Guy to the edge of a small, hedge-bordered field that lay just beyond the church. The field was piled high with brush, bits of old furniture, broken fruit crates—a familiar assortment of inflammable odds and ends.

"Blackhope's getting ready for Guy Fawkes Day," I observed.

Guy looked mildly surprised. "You know about Guy Fawkes, do you?"

"Remember, remember, the fifth of November," I chanted. "The fifth of November, 1605, to be precise when Catholic conspirators tried, and failed, to blow up Parliament with thirty-six barrels of gunpowder"—I took a breath—"an event which is commemorated unto this day by bonfires and general carousing."

"I am impressed," said Guy.

"My husband singed his eyebrows lightning the bonfire in our village last year." I turned to look out over the valley. "This is a great location. If the weather clears, Blackhope's bonfire'll be seen from one end of the valley to the other."

"It will also be seen from Wyrdhurst Hall." Guy pointed to a dark blur of trees a mile or so up the valley.

If I squinted, I could just make out the tops of the hall's twin towers. "Are Blackhope's women sending Jared a message?" I quipped. "I'll bet they'd like to light a fire under him."

Guy didn't crack a smile. "I presume Mrs. Hollander informed you of her husband's dissatisfaction with the local charwomen."

I nodded. "I imagine they were pretty ticked off."

"They were. But the selection of this place for the bonfire has a more complicated history." Guy drew a hand through the air, outlining a rectangle within the small field. "A schoolhouse once stood here. It burned to the ground in October

1917. The schoolmaster burned to death in it." He jutted his chin toward the church. "There's a tablet on the south wall, commemorating his death. It was paid for by the people of Blackhope. He was greatly loved, you see."

"Poor soul," I said.

Guy kicked at a chair leg that had fallen free from the tangle of brush. "The villagers blamed Josiah Byrd for the schoolmaster's death. Several had seen Josiah leaving the schoolhouse shortly before the fire started. Nothing was ever proved, but the villagers believed that Josiah had gotten away with murder."

I looked from the rain-soaked kindling to Wyrdhurst's gray stone towers and felt a chill seep through me. Had Edward been the schoolteacher, Claire his besotted pupil? Would Josiah kill a man to prevent an unsuitable match?

"What was the schoolmaster's name?" I inquired.

"Clive," said Guy. "Clive Eccles Aynsworth."

I tore my gaze from the twin towers and relaxed. In hindsight, my scenario seemed faintly ridiculous. As a privileged young woman, Claire would have been educated at home by governesses. She would have had little, if any, contact with the schoolmaster.

"Why would Josiah want to murder a schoolteacher?" I asked.

"No one knows," Guy replied. "Josiah had a foul temper and a tyrannical nature. The villagers may have simply wanted him to be guilty of the crime."

I smiled ruefully. I felt exactly the same way about Jared.

Guy carried on with his story. "The villagers couldn't bring Josiah to justice—he was far too rich and powerful—

so they found another way to punish him. They built the Guy Fawkes bonfire on the burnt-out remains of the schoolhouse, where it could be seen from Wyrdhurst Hall."

"Did Josiah get the message?" I asked.

"He closed the hall the following spring," Guy replied. "He returned to Newcastle and was never again seen at Wyrdhurst."

"Until he was buried there." I looked again toward the gray towers and asked, "Was Josiah's daughter interred at Wyrdhurst?"

"I don't know," said Guy. "Why do you ask?"

"I'm just trying to figure out why a guy who could afford to be buried anywhere would choose to be buried where everyone hated his guts." I shrugged. "Maybe he wanted to be near his daughter. He must have loved her."

"I'm sure he did." Guy pulled his collar up against the stiffening breeze.

I turned to him. "How do you know so much about Clive Aynsworth's alleged murder?"

"The story resurfaced when the hall was restored," Guy informed me. "Someone revived the tradition of building the bonfire where the schoolhouse once stood. Someone placed flowers before Mr. Aynsworth's tablet. Someone resurrected the tale of Josiah's guilty ghost." He gazed at me intently. "Someone resents Wyrdhurst and all who dwell there."

"Including *me?*" I said, after a beat. "Do you think a *villager* caused my accident?"

"Not directly. Not intentionally." Guy glanced skyward. "Let's return to the car, shall we? The wind's becoming a bit brisk."

"I don't care if it snows!" I cried. "I'm not going anywhere until you tell me what you know."

"I don't know anything . . . yet." Guy looked down at the graveled lane. "The theory linking Jared Hollander to the Wyrdhurst ghost is worth exploring. But Mr. Hollander isn't the only one who might want to impersonate the late and unlamented Josiah Byrd."

I stared hard at his chiseled profile. "Go on."

"Jared Hollander has installed a more-than-adequate security system in Wyrdhurst," Guy said, "but Mrs. Hollander seldom remembers to use it. If someone wished to enter the hall covertly, he would be wise to do so while Mr. Hollander was absent."

"That would explain why weird things happened when Nicole's alone." I nodded thoughtfully. "I'm with you so far."

"Your accident occurred on a military road that cuts across the Byrd estate," Guy continued. "At its closest point, it comes within a quarter-mile of Wyrdhurst Hall. If someone wished to enter Wyrdhurst through the back door, so to speak, he might take the road you inadvertently took."

"And leave the gate open in the process," I said.

"Precisely."

"Let me see if I've got this straight." I paused to marshal my thoughts before summarizing: "You think a villager has been using a military road to sneak into Wyrdhurst Hall in order to frighten Josiah's great-granddaughter as a sort of delayed retribution for the murder of Clive Aynsworth." I felt slightly winded by the time I concluded, "That's why the gate was left open. And that's why I nearly died."

"It may have noting to do with Mr. Aynsworth's murder," Guy allowed. "All of it—the bonfire, the flowers, the so-called haunting—may be part of an elaborate prank, meant to encourage Mrs. Hollander to vacate her ancestral home."

"Why would anyone want Nicole to—" I broke off as the answer came to me. "Because if Nicole leaves, Jared'll go with her, and it'd kill Jared to leave Wyrdhurst."

"A fitting punishment," Guy commented. "Mr. Hollander should have thought twice before insulting the local charwomen."

I ran a hand through my hair. "Do you think the villager will give up, now that the road's washed out?"

"Only one access point is washed out," Guy corrected. "Several others are still in good order."

I gave Guy a sidelong glance. "Do you have a suspect in mind?"

"Not yet," he said.

"That's what the song and dance was for, right?" I jerked a thumb in the direction of the pub. "You're using Bart Little as a public-address system. You want him to let the villagers know that you're keeping an eye on them."

"That's the general idea," Guy conceded.

I tucked my hands into my jacket pockets and gazed speculatively at Her Majesty's rooftop. "Bart was awfully quick to mention the ghost, wasn't he? He seemed to get a kick out of trying to spook me." I bumped the captain with my elbow. "Maybe *he's* haunting Wyrdhurst."

"He's no more likely then the next man," said Guy.

"I'll bet the whole family's in on it," I said, warming to my theory. "That's why James wouldn't look at me, why Bart offered me free meals." I snapped my fingers. "That's why Brett and Bert were so uncomfortable when I thanked them. They're feeling *guilty* for causing my crash."

"Let's not get ahead of ourselves," Guy cautioned. "It's merely an alternative hypothesis."

"Crumbs," I said, crestfallen. "I was all set to sink my teeth into Jared."

"There's no reason to rule him out," said Guy. "I intend to follow every lead."

I scuffed my heel in the gravel. "Does that include Adam? Is that why you ran a background check on him?"

Guy gave a long-suffering groan. "Contrary to popular belief, I don't spend my days vetting civilians. I did not run a background check on Mr. Chase."

"Who called his editor?" I asked.

"Not a glimmer." Guy contemplated the clearing sky. "When the editor refused—very wisely—to give information over the telephone, the caller rang off. Most interesting . . ." He turned to me. "But nothing for you to concern yourself with. To answer your question, I haven't investigated Mr. Chase, because I've no reason to suspect him of anything."

"I knew it," I crowed.

"That being said," Guy continued, "I would still caution you against confiding in him."

"Why?" I asked.

"I suspect that Mr. Chase knows more about the Wyrdhurst ghost than he's willing to let on," Guy answered. "He's a writer, he's trained to observe, and he seems to enjoy chatting up the villagers. If there's a plot afoot in Blackhope, I'll wager that Mr. Chase knows all about it."

I though instantly of Mr. Garnett, the talkative mechanic who'd told Adam about Josiah's ghost, but just as quickly brushed the thought aside. I refused to believe that Adam would conceal information about my accident. Adam cared about me. If he knew who'd left the gate open, he'd step forward.

"May I tell Nicole about Bart Little?" I asked.

"I'd rather you didn't," said Guy. "Not until I've had a chance to eliminate her husband from my inquiries."

A novel idea popped into my head. "Maybe they're all at it—Jared, Bart, James, Brett, and Bert. What a joke."

"There's nothing remotely humorous about harassing a vulnerable young woman." Guy surveyed the village as fiercely as a hawk scouting for prey. "I fully intend to put a stop to it." He turned to me. "And I need your help."

Plucky women long for action. I was, alas, consigned to observation. On the way back to Wyrdhurst Hall, Guy gave me my instructions.

I was to keep an eye on Nicole. Period. I was forbidden to search Wyrdhurst for signs of illicit activity or to ask the villagers leading questions. I was absolutely forbidden to approach, apprehend, or otherwise confront anyone. If I saw anything suspicious I was to ring Guy at once. He offered me a spare cell phone, but I told him that Bill had already replaced the one lost in the crash.

"I'll have men posted on the ground," he told me, "with orders to keep well out of sight of the hall. I'd like to post men inside Wyrdhurst, but Mr. Hollander wouldn't permit it."

I hesitated briefly before asking, "Won't your men wonder why you're taking such an interest in Wyrdhurst Hall?"

"I'm investigating the misuse of a military road," Guy replied. "Your accident gave me all the cause I need to take an interest in Wyrdhurst Hall."

I smiled thinly. "Glad to oblige."

As we drew up beneath the porte cochere, Guy said, "I have no right to ask for your help in this matter, Lori. I know that you have your own work to do."

"My work isn't important," I assured him. "Nicole's peace of mind is. I can always extend my stay."

Bill would understand, I told myself. And Adam would be delighted.

CHAPTER

13

The brown-paper-wrapped parcel was still waiting for me when I went up to the red room, but now Reginald sat beside it, as if insisting that I give it my full attention.

I hung my jacket in the wardrobe, kicked off my damp boots, and climbed onto the bed, knocking Reginald to the floor in the process. Instead of picking him up, I reached for Teddy and placed him on the bed beside me.

"It's either a big cell phone," I told the bear, as I tore into the brown paper, "or a small phone in a big package. Either way it's—" I broke off, my jaw dropping, as the last of the paper fell away.

Bill hadn't sent a cell phone. He'd sent a blank-paged journal bound in a dark-blue leather.

"Aunt Dimity?" I blinked for a moment, too stunned to

speak, then threw back my head and laughed out loud. "Well, Teddy," I said, "now Wyrdhurst Hall is truly haunted."

Dimity Westwood had been my late mother's closest friend and my greatest benefactress. She'd bestowed a considerable fortune upon me as well as the honey-colored cottage I now called home. She'd been dead for just over half a decade, but her death hadn't kept her from taking an interest in me.

Long after her mortal remains had dwindled into dust, Aunt Dimity kept in touch. When I opened the blue journal, her handwriting appeared, filling the blank pages with sound advice, pithy observations and treasured words of wisdom. It was because of Dimity that I had no fear of otherworldly spirits. She was the most benign of entities, rarely intruding without invitation, seeking only to help.

I felt a pleasant thrill of anticipation as I sat cross-legged on the bed, with the blue journal open on my knees.

"Dimity?" I said. "What brings you to Wyrdhurst?"

The blank page came alive with the familiar curving lines of royal-blue ink, curling and looping in an elegant copperplate that put Edward's undisciplined scrawl to shame.

Lori, you must leave this place at once.

"Don't be silly," I said, pulling Teddy closer. "I like it here. And I've got a job to do. Two jobs, really. First, there's the evaluation of the—"

I don't care if you have two dozen jobs to do. You must leave immediately.

I stared at Dimity's words, taken aback by her vehemence. She didn't usually order me about.

You don't seem to realize the effect the hall is having on you. The handwriting paused. *When did you last speak with Bill?*

I thought for a moment. "Yesterday," I said finally. "Just after I arrived."

There you are. You've been here all day today and you haven't once rung your husband.

"He knows where I am," I reminded her.

That's not the point.

"What is the point?" I said, a bit heatedly.

You aren't yourself. You're being influenced by the hall's occupant to behave shamefully.

"Shamefully?" I was shocked by the accusation. "I haven't done anything shameful."

You will if you don't depart promptly. I should have known this would happen. I blame myself.

"Dimity," I said, "you have nothing to blame yourself for. And you certainly have no reason to blame me. I haven't done anything except forget to call Bill."

But why have you forgotten to call him? I suspect it's because you've had someone else on your mind. Another man, perhaps? A very young man with dark eyes and dark hair, who

"He's not all that young," I interrupted. "I'd say he's closing in on forty—a very *fit* forty."

Ah.

There was a faint buzzing in my ears and my head began to swim.

You must do as I say, Lori. I'm here to help you. I won't let anything hurt you.

Aunt Dimity's handwriting seemed to waver, then float from the page, smudging the air in a drift of faded blue streamers. I dropped the journal and pressed my hands to my temples. The room was intolerably stuffy, the air so stale I could scarcely breathe. Dazed, I stumbled to the windows and threw one open.

The drapes billowed around me and the bed curtains flapped, but the sharp breeze cleared my head as quickly as a bucket of ice water. I clutched the bars briefly, to steady myself, then turned to gaze resentfully at the journal.

Aunt Dimity was spouting nonsense. She seemed to think that Nicole, the "hall's occupant," had pushed me into Adam's arms, but nothing could be further from the truth. My hostess had tried her best to steer me away from Adam. Everyone—Nicole, Guy, and now Dimity—was trying to steer me away from Adam. Even Reginald seemed to look at me with a faint air of reproach.

I was sick of being bullied. I wasn't a child. No one had a right to tell me who could or couldn't be my friend.

I scooped up the blue journal and Reginald and shut them both in the wardrobe, kissed the tip of Teddy's nose, and returned him to the bedside table. In my haste, I managed to knock over the framed photograph of my family. I barely noticed as it clattered to the floor.

The library doors opened so easily that I nearly fell into the room. Hatch, I presumed, had finally brought his oilcan to bear on the sticky hinges.

I made a beeline for the oak table, but stopped short, frowning. Before leaving to have lunch with Captain Manning, I'd placed the gray ledger on top of Edward's notes. Now it lay to one side, next to the inscribed copy of *Shuttleworth's Birds*.

I sat in the wooden armchair and looked through the

notes. They, too, had been rearranged. When I'd left, the message mentioning Edith Ann had been buried deep in the pile. Now it sat atop the stack.

I doubted that the Hatches had interfered with my work. They'd been given strict orders to leave the library alone. Nicole, on the other hand, had free rein to examine anything she pleased. It seemed likely that she'd filled the afternoon's empty hours by reading Edward's words.

I wondered what she made of them. She seemed to know little and care less about her great-aunt. Claire was to her a dim and distant figure who'd died without accomplishing much. I hoped the notes had changed her mind, had touched her as deeply as they'd touched me. To me, Claire was a living, breathing girl who'd loved a boy despite her father's disapproval. A life filled with such passion, however brief, could not be meaningless.

I made a mental note to ask Nicole if she'd spent the afternoon at the oak table, switched on the reading lamps, and opened the gray ledger.

The first entry was dated July 21, 1914, when, presumably, Josiah had received his first shipment of books. The last entry was dated September 4, 1917. The cataloguer had been thorough, conscientiously recording pertinent details about each book, but he hadn't been Edward. The anonymous librarian's handwriting was precise, meticulous, neither cramped nor sprawling, and highly legible—nothing like Edward's unruly scribbles.

I closed the ledger, set it aside, and began the laborious task of repacking the wooden crate. I could have left the chore to Hatch, but I wanted to touch the books again before they were returned to their dusty outpost in the east tower.

As I slid each volume into place, I felt a lingering sense of dissatisfaction. It was as if an important fact had passed before my eyes unseen and now lurked in a dim corner of my brain, awaiting recognition. The harder I chased after it, the more elusive the fact became.

My mind soon rebelled against the strain and began to wander. My first three days in Northumberland had been nothing if not eventful. I'd had a close brush with death, awakened in the arms of a beautiful stranger, unearthed a compelling love story, and been recruited by the army to help in its inquiries. If my speculations held water, I'd also been ambushed by an evil man bent on driving his young wife insane.

I wondered how Aubrey Shuttleworth would have illustrated such a remarkable chain of events. Smiling, I took up *Shuttleworth's Birds* and leafed through it, pausing to admire the illustrations and reread the verse. I'd just reached a splendid portrait of a stooping kestrel when the library doors swung open and Nicole pranced into the room. She seemed very pleased with herself.

"You look like the cat who got the cream," I observed. "What have you been up to?"

"I drove to Alnwick." Her voice had a defiant ring to it, as if she'd intentionally broken one of her husband's many rules. "Have you been to Alnwick Castle? It's like something out of a fairy tale. They call it the Windsor of the north, you know, and I can see why. The red drawing room is an absolute jewel, and the library . . ." She dragged a chair over and sat with her elbows on the table. "The library's the most beautiful room I've ever seen. You really must have a peep at it before you leave Northumberland. The guides are absolute angels."

"I'll bear that in mind." I was glad that Nicole hadn't let Guy's defection spoil her day. "Were you in Alnwick all afternoon?"

"I left after lunch," she said. "Jared won't be pleased—he doesn't like me driving on my own—but I don't care. I simply had to get away from Wyrdhurst."

"Why?" I asked quickly. "Did something happen?"

Nicole's laughter rang like a tinkling bell. "Boredom happened, that's all. I suppose I should be grateful. It's a pleasant change of pace from abject terror."

If Nicole had spent the afternoon at Alnwick Castle, she couldn't have moved the ledger or examined Edward's notes. I was about to ask if Mrs. Hatch had been in to dust the library when Nicole sent me veering in an entirely different direction.

"What've you got there?" she said, looking down at the stooping kestrel. "A children's book?"

It was as if a flare had gone off in the room. The elusive fact I'd been chasing suddenly flashed across my mind in neon letters. I looked from the kestrel to the books in the wooden crate and whispered, "Edith Ann . . ."

"Pardon?" said Nicole.

I was too blinded by insight to respond. Why hadn't I seen it sooner?

Shuttleworth's Birds was a children's book. Claire must have had dozens like it. Fairy tales, fables, and Arthurian romances had been all the rage during her Edwardian childhood.

And one of the best-loved children's writers of the period was a slightly crack-brained woman named Edith Ann Malson.

Malson's books had long been out of fashion, but Stan

Finderman had acquired a few copies for the juvenilia section of the university's rare-book department. I remembered the day he'd shown them to me.

"Malson was a nutcase," he acknowledged, pulling a volume from a high shelf. "But kids loved her. Kids always love sick jokes. See here? Monmouth Mouse and Romney Rat go to a natural history museum in Sussex. Monmouth thinks he recognizes a cousin in one of the displays. Turns out that his cousin *is* one of the displays."

I could see the illustration as clearly as if the book were open before me: the stuffed cousin, Monmouth's horrified recoil, Romney's solicitous paw on Monmouth's shoulder. The story ended happily—they smuggle the cousin out of the museum and give him a decent burial—but Malson's gruesome sense of humor, though endearing to children, had proved unpopular with modern parents. Successive generations scarcely knew her name.

I groaned softly, chagrined that it had taken me so long to put two and two together. Edward had assured Claire that "Edith Ann" would carry his letters to her while he was gone. I was willing to bet that he'd arranged to have his letters smuggled into Wyrdhurst, hidden in seemingly innocuous copies of Edith Ann Malson's works. Claire, for her part, would have shelved Malson's books unobtrusively with the rest of the juvenilia in the hall.

I glanced at the hollowed-out copy of *Ivanhoe* in which Claire had hidden Edward's notes. If I could locate the children's books in Wyrdhurst Hall, I felt certain that Malson's works—and possibly Edward's letters—would be with them.

I silently blessed Edith Ann Malson's name. She'd given

me the perfect excuse to search Wyrdhurst Hall. If I happened to find evidence of human intruders in the process, so much the better.

"Nicole," I said, turning to my young friend, "could I interest you in a treasure hunt?"

CHAPTER

14

Nicole was entranced by my tale of her great-aunt's grand passion. She handled each scribbled note as if it were holy writ, and choked up when she read the inscription in *Shuttleworth's Birds.*

"Just twelve years old," she said, with a tremulous sigh. "I wonder if she was already in love with Edward when he gave the book to her, or if friendship turned to love as she grew older?"

"She couldn't have been more than twenty when she died," I chimed in. "He must have been her first love and her last."

Nicole put the book aside and wiped her eyes. "She never seemed real to me before. It must have taken enormous courage to defy Josiah."

"And here we are, defying him again, just by talking about

Claire and Edward." I glanced over my shoulder at the portrait. "Do you ever get the feeling that he's watching you?"

"Constantly." Nicole gazed intently at Josiah. "There's
something about his eyes, so fixed and full of disapproval."

"I'm sure he wouldn't approve of us looking for Edward's letters," I said. "I'm afraid Jared might feel the same
way. It's not really what I came here to do."

"It's what *I* want you to do," Nicole replied stoutly. "If
Jared objects—"

"He may not object," I temporized. "A complete run of
Edith Ann Malson would be worth a pretty penny at auction.
Collectors froth at the mouth when they come up for sale."

"Money," Nicole said darkly, "is the one thing my husband
understands." She got to her feet. "But if he so much as men-
tions selling Miss Malson's books, I'll . . . I'll become *very
cross.*"

I was both disconcerted and greatly cheered by Nicole's
boldness. The alarm-free night and the solo journey to Alnwick Castle had evidently awakened her independent spirit.
I had a sneaking suspicion that Jared would come home to
find a full-blown rebellion on his hands.

If, I reminded myself, he'd left Wyrdhurst to begin with.

Nicole's newfound self-confidence proved to be a double-
edged sword. I was glad she'd found the strength to stand up
to her husband, less pleased when she stood up to me.

Over dinner, she firmly vetoed my suggestion that we
begin looking for Malson's books at once, then badgered me
into retiring at an absurdly early hour.

"I'm just as eager to find Edward's letters as you are,"

she lectured, "but we musn't forget Dr. MacEwan's sensible advice. If he wants you well rested, then well rested you shall be."

One can't be well rested with food half digested. The rhyme tripped through my mind as I climbed into bed less than an hour after gorging myself shamelessly on a succulent saddle of lamb and devouring more than my fair share of Claire's Lace. Once under the blankets, I tossed and turned restlessly, regretting my overindulgence, until my thoughts strayed to plans for tomorrow.

Where would we find Malson's books? There was no need to search the east tower. Hatch had assured us that the only books there had been the ones in the wooden crate. The juvenilia must have been stored separately. Perhaps, I thought, they'd been crated and left where they'd once been read: in the nursery.

I turned my head and looked past Major Ted's stalwart silhouette to the barred windows. What had Dr. MacEwan told me? The nursery, he'd said, would have been upstairs, where "the kiddies' bawling" wouldn't disturb the parents.

A nursery would be easy enough to recognize. All I had to do was look for another room with barred windows. Nicole would thank me if I located the letters. Guy would thank me if I found evidence of intruders. My tummy would thank me for giving it a chance to walk off the heavy meal.

I flung back the covers and hopped out of bed. When it came to being a strong, determined woman, Nicole had nothing on me.

———

I felt like a cat burglar, sidling furtively down the corridor, garbed in black turtleneck, jeans, and sneakers, Nicole's flashlight clutched firmly in one hand, the other cupped around its lens to keep the beam from giving me away.

Wyrdhurst was as silent as a tomb. I heard no creaks, no moaning wind, and the only audible footsteps were the sneaker-muted ones I made myself. If Jared was lurking in the upper stories, he was doing so discreetly.

I paused at the main staircase to peer downward. The light in the entrance hall had been extinguished and I saw no sign of life. Nicole and the Hatches were, I hoped, in bed and sleeping soundly.

Satisfied that my self-appointed guardian wouldn't catch me prowling after curfew, I dropped my cupped hand from the flashlight and started up the stairs. I'd climbed no more than three steps when a faint sound caught at the edge of my hearing.

It came from below. I thought at first it was the high-pitched whistle of a distant teakettle and wondered if Mrs. Hatch was in the kitchen, brewing a late-night cuppa. It took a moment for me to realize that the unearthly, piercing shrieks came from a human throat.

The blood froze in my veins. For a moment I couldn't move. Then I was sprinting down the stairs, shouting, "Nicole! Nicole, where are you?"

The screams went on and on and I raced after them, plunging through the dining room, the billiards room, the study, crashing into tables, chairs, and shelves of bric-a-brac, leaving a trail of destruction in my wake.

The study doors stood open and the library was dimly

lit. I barreled straight into the room, rumpling the Turkish carpets as I skidded to a halt. Nicole sat facing the windows, her spine rigid, her nails biting into the oak table, shrieks streaming from her gaping mouth.

I tore across the room, pulled her from the chair, and spun her around.

"Nicole," I ordered. "Stop it."

Her mouth opened wide, but no sound came out. She seemed not to recognize me.

"It's Lori," I said. "Don't be afraid."

Nicole drew a wavering breath. "The w-window . . . I s-saw . . ."

"Tell me what you saw."

"It *flew*," she breathed, and folded at the knees like a rag doll.

She was as light as a sparrow. I carried her to the sofa and covered her with the cashmere blanket that had, just the day before, covered me. A brief phone call roused the Hatches, who came quickly, clad in flannel robes and slippers. Mrs. Hatch brought brandy, Hatch the mobile telephone. He'd already summoned Dr. MacEwan.

I called Guy.

"There's been another incident," I told him. "Nicole saw something outside the library. She's shaken, but Dr. MacEwan's on his way. I'm going out to—"

"You'll do no such thing." Guy seemed preternaturally calm, a prim professor offering a mild rebuke. "You'll stay with Mrs. Hollander."

"But—"

"It's too late," Guy interjected. "Whoever was there is

long gone. You're to stay with Mrs. Hollander and leave the rest to me. Please."

The final, gruff monosyllable was all that kept me from tossing the phone aside and dashing out into the night. I glanced at the prone figure on the sofa, swallowed my frustration, and agreed, reluctantly to follow orders.

"Let me know if you find anything," I said. "I want this sick joker locked up."

"He will be, Lori. He will be."

The next few hours passed in a blur. Nicole drifted in and out of consciousness, babbled incoherently about flying ghosts, and became hysterical when Dr. MacEwan suggested taking her to her room. She finally wound up in my bed, heavily sedated.

After the doctor had gone, I tucked Teddy in with Nicole, then paced the room, too furious to sleep. It was so unfair. Nicole had just begun to try her wings. Now she lay in a fetal curl, half out of her mind with fear. I laid my hand on her feverish forehead, then went to the windows to peer out into the darkness.

Guy had been right to rein me in. If I ever caught the devil who was tormenting Nicole, I'd wring his neck.

CHAPTER

It was past midnight before I dropped into a fitful doze on the fainting couch. Mrs. Hatch arrived at eight, with breakfast on a tray, and Dr. MacEwan showed up at nine to check on his newest patient, who had not yet wakened from her drug-induced slumber. When he'd finished his examination, I accompanied him to the front door.

"Mrs. Hollander thinks she's seen a ghost flitting about outside the library windows," the doctor informed me. "Daft, of course, but there you are. I don't want her left alone. Have you notified her husband?"

I shook my head. "I don't know where to reach him, and he didn't leave a number with the Hatches."

Dr. MacEwan scowled as I opened the front door. "The great lump. He's no more use than a headache. He'd be no use at all to his wife, in her present condition." He snorted scornfully and trotted down the stairs, promising to return later in the day.

Mrs. Hatch volunteered to remain with Nicole, so I left them in my room and returned to the library. I felt restless and unsettled, impatient for action or for news that some action had been taken.

Had Guy's men combed the tangled garden for clues during the night? Had they searched the terrace? Had they found fingerprints, footprints, a telltale tuft of wool caught on a thorny bush? I went to the windows and peered closely at the garden, but saw no sign that anyone had been there.

I turned my attention to the oak table, where Edward's notes lay in disarray. Nicole had evidently been rereading them when she'd been so rudely interrupted. I sat where she'd been sitting, straightened the scattered sheets, and watched in startled amazement as a bar of sunlight fell across my hand. Delighted, I lifted my gaze and looked straight into Adam's eyes.

He stood at the central window, dressed in a lightweight anorak, black jeans, and the cobalt-blue ribbed sweater I'd first seen by firelight in the fishing hut. As he raised his wrist to tap his watch, the mantelpiece clock chimed ten.

"Oh, jeez," I muttered, mortified. Our outing to the Devil's Ring had slipped my mind.

I jumped up, pointed to my left, and met him at a tall, glass-paned door that had been hidden by the rotting drapes. He brought a bracing breeze with him as he entered the room.

"I tried the bellpull," he explained, "but no one answered. I somehow knew I'd find you here. Are you ready?"

"I will be," I promised. "Don't move."

By venturing out of the hall, I was, strictly speaking, dis-obeying Guy's orders, but the thought of sunlight on my face was irresistible—it seemed an age since I'd last seen a cloud-less sky. I dashed upstairs to grab my jacket and change into hiking boots, told Mrs. Hatch I'd be gone for a few hours, and, as an afterthought, pocketed Nicole's cell phone, in case Guy called.

Adam was standing at the oak table when I returned.

"Are these the notes you mentioned?" he asked. "Ed-ward's notes to Claire?"

"Yes," I said. "I'll tell you all about them, but let's get out of here first, before someone tries to stop us."

"You sound as if you're being held against your will," Adam commented as he stepped onto the terrace.

"I've got bars on my bedroom windows, don't I?" I pulled the door shut and paused with my hand on the latch.

"Forget something?" Adam asked.

"No," I said, perplexed. "It's the door. Nicole never told me about it. It was hidden by the drapes and I don't remem-ber noticing it before. So how did I know it was there?"

"You made a logical assumption," said Adam. "Where there's a terrace, there must be a door."

"Right." I stared at the door a moment longer before turning my face to the sun and saying, "I'll race you to the mausoleum."

"You're on," said Adam, and he took off, with me chasing after him, both of us laughing like children.

We strode side by side across the rolling plateau, following a path that was little more than a groove cut into the sheep-cropped turf. A brisk wind flattened the dried grasses bordering the path, and powder-puff clouds scattered shadows across an endless expanse of hills. The view was spectacular, the clear light almost dazzling, but the land wasn't as open as it had at first appeared to be.

We'd gone no more than fifty yards beyond the mausoleum when the path dipped into a fold that hid the house from sight. It seemed to me that an intruder using the path would find it easy to approach Wyrdhurst undetected, and he could do so without leaving a trace. The wind-scoured ground was too hard to give up footprints, there were no thorny shrubs to catch at clothing, and the brittle grasses were already split and broken.

"Does this path meet up with the military track?" I asked.

Adam nodded, his dark curls tossing in the wind. "The track's a quarter-mile from here, as the crow flies. Will it bother you to see it?"

"Nope," I said. "I'd make a lousy poster child for post-traumatic stress."

"You fainted on the hidden staircase," Adam reminded me.

"Ancient history." I pursed my lips. "Which brings us to the fascinating conversation I had yesterday with Guy . . ."

Once I started talking, I couldn't stop. I spoke at breakneck speed, as if ridding myself of an unwanted burden of information. I started with Guy's unspoken feelings for Nicole and went straight through to my curtailed search for Edith Ann Malson's books. By the time we reached the military track, I'd filled Adam in on everything that had happened since I'd last seen him.

When I finished, I felt as light as a feather. I felt a bit

lightheaded, too, so intoxicated by the pure air that I swayed on my feet. Adam put out a hand to steady me, but I dodged past him and strutted confidently across the rutted track, to prove that I could face reminders of my crash without coming unglued.

"Your turn to talk," I said as we regained the path. "Tell me about the Devil's Ring."

"It's a neolithic stone circle," Adam began. "Northumberland is littered with them."

"What about artillery practice?" I said, alarmed. "Is the army allowed to destroy prehistoric sites?"

"If it weren't, it couldn't conduct exercises anywhere in Britain," Adam replied. "Ours is a very small island with a very crowded history. Preservation isn't always possible, but the Ring is safe enough. Its proximity to Wyrdhurst Hall protects it—and us."

"Why is it called the Devil's Ring?" I asked.

"I've heard a dozen explanations," Adam said. "My favorite goes something like this: those who enter the Ring must be pure of heart or risk losing their immortal souls to the devil."

I felt a twinge of apprehension, but chose to ignore it. I refused to let a morbid superstition cast a shadow on our perfect day. Forcing a laugh, I linked arms with Adam and demanded, in a mock-solemn tone of voice, "Are you feeling pure of heart today, my son?"

Adam favored me with an enticing, sidelong glance before answering, "Not entirely." He put his hand over mine, drew in a deep breath, and let it out in a satisfied rush. "I'm glad you suggested the walk. I haven't been to the Ring in ages. It's a special place."

"Edward and Claire thought so." As the words left my lips, my head began to spin and I stopped short, clutching Adam's arm for support.

"You're tired," he said firmly. He motioned toward a grassy rise some twenty yards to our right. "We can rest out of the wind over there."

"Rest? Who needs rest?" I shook off the dizzy spell, shot past him, and scrambled to the top of the hillock, where I raised my arms in victory, only to let them fall slowly to my sides. "Adam," I called, peering curiously down the far side of the hill. "Come and see what I've found."

He clambered up the slope to stand beside me.

I looked at him uncertainly. "Is it the Devil's Ring?"

"No," he replied. "But I'm damned if I know what it is."

Below us, at the bottom of the long, narrow hill, lay a complex formation of rocks. The rocks were small enough to carry, too large to blow away, and they'd been arranged in regular lines to form squares, rectangles, and an enormous half-circle. The manner in which the shapes intersected and connected reminded me of Scara Brae, a many-chambered Stone Age village I'd once visited, up in the Orkney Islands.

"Scara Brae," I said, "writ large."

Adam understood the reference. "They do look like rooms," he agreed. "But the formation's not neolithic. It wasn't here the last time I visited the Ring."

"Are you sure?" I glanced over my shoulder. "It's pretty well concealed from the path."

Adam conceded the point, but remained perplexed. "Why would someone build a Stone Age village?"

"Maybe it's not a Stone Age village," I reasoned. "We're

on army property. It's probably something to do with military exercises."

"You may be right." Adam squatted to scrabble in the dirt at my feet. When he stood, he held six shiny brass cartridge cases in his palm.

"Do not handle military debris," I pronounced. "It may explode and kill you." I looked askance at the cartridges. "Kind of small for artillery, aren't they?"

"A new secret weapon, no doubt." Adam smiled as he pocketed the cartridges.

"I'll ask Guy. He'll know." I turned a slow circle, savoring the moment. "You can see forever from up here. If we looked hard enough, I'll bet we could see Scara Brae."

"I don't know about Scara Brae," Adam said, "but we can certainly see the Ring."

He lifted his arm to point me in the right direction, but I'd already spotted the six gray stones that jutted like broken teeth from the tussocky ground.

I'd seen them before, in my dream.

The shock wave of recognition ripped me from my moorings. I felt an instant's giddiness and then everything came unglued. The blue sky seemed to ripple, colors tumbled and swirled, and the world seemed to slow on its axis. The chill wind gentled to a velvet breeze, dried grasses blew green and supple, and heather bloomed, cloaking the hills in soft clouds of lavender. The air was perfumed with the sweet scents of summer, warmed by a high summer sun, filled with the music of laughter and long-silent voices.

"You mustn't leave," I murmured. "You must never leave me."

I swayed again, on knees as weak as water, but when

Adam reached out to steady me this time, I turned into his arms and kissed him.

It wasn't a chaste kiss. It was the kind of kiss that leads to shameful things, but I felt no sense of shame. I was drunk on pure sensation, as if tasting for the first time the sweet, heady elixir of love. I twined my fingers in his curls, arched my back, and pressed myself against him, aching to feel once again every curve and hollow of the body that had shared its warmth with mine.

Then Adam was gripping my shoulders, hard, and pushing me away. "Lori," he managed. "Stop. It's not right."

I stood back, chastened. "Of course. Not here. We might be seen. Come on." And I started down the hill, toward the rock formation.

"Where are you going?" Adam called.

"To our place." I turned toward him. "We'll take the shortcut."

Adam approached me slowly, his troubled eyes never leaving my face. "Lori," he said softly, "how do you know about the shortcut?"

"Don't be a goose," I replied, smiling. "You showed it to me."

Adam shook his head. "We've never been here before. Not the two of us. Not together."

"But I . . ." The velvet breeze turned razor-sharp. "I remember . . ."

Adam cupped my face in his hands. "No."

The supple grasses shriveled and the lavender faded to brown. I backed away from Adam, looking wildly from side to side. "I *do* remember. Not just the shortcut, not just the terrace door . . ." A sharp pain lanced through my head and I crumpled, gasping, to the ground. "I knew where my room was. I turned down the corridor before Nicole told me which way to go. I *led* her to my room." I clenched my fists and pressed them to my temples. "I knew the dead animals didn't belong there. The room was a prison, not a zoo. Josiah put the bars in, to keep me from . . . to keep Claire from . . ." Adam dropped to his knees and I leaned into him, terrified. "I knew the books were hers *before* I found the notes. I *dreamt* of the Devil's Ring. Oh, Adam," I whimpered, "what's happening to me?"

"I don't know." He tightened his hold. "But I'm here, Lori. I won't let anything hurt you."

Through a haze of pain I seemed to see, in the stitches of his blue ribbed sweater, the loops and curls of royal-blue ink repeating the fierce, solemn promise: *I won't let anything hurt you.*

I buried my face in his sweater, whispering, *"Dimity . . ."*

CHAPTER

16

Adam all but carried me back to Wyrdhurst. I staggered along as best I could, but my mind was still half clouded, laced with memories that did not belong to me.

Adam asked no questions, demanded no explanations. He simply followed my faltering instructions, depositing me in his beat-up car, retrieving the blue journal from the wardrobe, and taking me away from Wyrdhurst Hall.

The farther we drove, the more coherent my thoughts became. By the time we reached the fishing hut, the pain in my head had subsided and the false memories had faded to dim shadows.

Adam guided me through the peacock-blue door, helped take off my jacket, and seated me in the leather armchair. While he got a fire going, I noted that the room had been put to rights. The narrow iron bed was back in its corner, the armchair cozily tucked to one side of the small hearth. Still, the hut seemed as familiar to me as my cottage, a safe place where I could recover from yet another accident.

Adam pulled a beechwood chair from the pine table and sat facing me across the hearth.

I must have looked haggard, and I felt as fragile as a teacup, as if a single misstep would shatter me. Tears welled in my eyes as I told him, quite firmly, "I'm not crazy."

"I know."

"What I'm about to do will *seem* crazy"—my voice broke and a tear spilled down my cheek—"but it's *not*."

"I believe you."

I swiped the tears away and opened the blue journal.

"I'm sorry, Dimity," I said. "I'm so sorry. You tried to warn me, but I wouldn't listen."

As the elegant copperplate curled across the page, a sense of calm came over me. Dimity's love was like a fortress, shielding me from harm. Nothing evil could touch me, so long as she was near.

Tell me what happened, my dear.

"It's been happening for a while, but I didn't realize it until today." I took a deep breath. "I have memories and . . . and feelings that don't belong to me. It's as if . . . someone else . . . is in my head."

Someone else IS in your head, my dear. As I told you before, you're not yourself.

Dimity's literal use of the commonplace phrase provoked a ragged chuckle.

The handwriting continued. *You're not entirely yourself, at any rate. It's my fault, I'm afraid. Your relationship with me has* made you vulnerable. Once the door is opened between the living and the dead, there's no telling who will come through. We're not all of us charming, sensible, and sane, you know. Some of us are quite mad.

"Are you telling me . . . ?" I paused, momentarily at a loss for words. I'd always regarded Dimity's presence in my life as a blessing. It had never occurred to me that it might also be a liability. "Do you mean to say that any passing noncorporeal being can just walk in and take up residence in my head?"

Not exactly. Have you been unwell since your arrival at Wyrdhurst Hall? Dizziness, headaches, queasiness?

"All three," I admitted.

I thought as much. You've always been a stubborn girl, Lori, and admirably independent. No one could enter your mind without a struggle. Hence the headaches.

"Who's inside my mind?" I asked, though I was already fairly certain of the answer.

Someone called Claire.

"Claire Byrd?"

She doesn't use a last name, but if "Claire Byrd" means something to you, it's undoubtedly she. You've taken an interest in this Claire Byrd, I presume.

"A great interest," I acknowledged.

Influenced, no doubt, by Claire herself. She's been working on you ever since you entered Wyrdhurst. That's why I insisted on joining you. I felt the bond between us waver alarmingly. Other bonds wavered as well, I'll wager.

My conscience burned as I recalled the framed photograph of my beloved boys, clattering to the floor. "Marriage and motherhood," I murmured. "How could I, Dimity? How could I forget my family?"

You must blame yourself, Lori. Claire's a very clever, very desperate girl.

"Why did she choose me?" I demanded. "The woman who lives in Wyrdhurst isn't nearly as bullheaded as I am. Why didn't Claire go after Nicole?"

Is Nicole a virgin?

"I think so."

Claire has a great need to express physical affection. She'd find it difficult to use an inexperienced woman. In Nicole's case, ignorance truly has been bliss.

You, on the other hand, have a passionate nature and the experience to go with it. You also have, if you'll forgive me, a roving eye. I take it there's an attractive man on hand?

I looked over my shoulder at Adam, who was quietly making tea, and remembered the warm flush that had spread through me as I gazed upon his face in the firelight, well before I'd set foot in Wyrdhurst Hall. Aunt Dimity was right. I did have a roving eye. It was part of my passionate nature. Claire had chosen her puppet wisely.

"His name's Adam," I said, under my breath. "Adam Chase. He saved my life."

Claire could use such a connection for her own purposes. Did she attempt to express herself through you?

The breathless moment on the moors came back to me in a vivid, visceral rush. I felt the heat rise again, and the hunger, and the helpless sense of losing him forever.

You're slow in answering, Lori. Perhaps I should restate the question more explicitly. Did Claire make use of your bond with Adam to express her own physical desires?

"She did. I threw myself at Adam. He stopped me before

things got out of hand, but if it hadn't been for him . . ." I groaned softly and hung my head.

Let's not become melodramatic, my dear. Do you think you're the first married woman to be distracted by a pretty face? Distraction is not action. You might have looked at Adam Chase, but you would never have touched him if it hadn't been for Claire. The shame is hers, not yours.

While Adam resumed his seat, there was a pause, as if Dimity were pondering her next words. Then the handwriting continued.

Claire is, alas, deeply troubled. I sense heartache, yes, but also anger, and an ardent desire to right a wrong. She's terribly concerned about the fate of a dark-haired, dark-eyed young man. That's why she drove your family from your mind. She wanted you to focus solely on one man.

How well she succeeded, I reflected. I'd been drawn to Adam from the start, but I hadn't become obsessed with him until I'd entered the hall. Aloud, I said, "She must be worried about Edward."

Whoever it is, I would counsel you to leave Wyrdhurst and never return. It's much the safest course.

Aunt Dimity's suggestion was tempting. Claire had entered my mind uninvited. She'd tampered with my dreams and taken advantage of my weaknesses. She'd blurred memories of my children and replaced my love for Bill with a fantasy of her own devising. I should have resented her, but I couldn't.

I turned toward the fire and saw in the leaping flames a young girl torn between her father's wishes and the dictates of her own heart. I admired her courage, understood her fears, and felt with every fiber of my being the depth of her love for Edward. For better or for worse, Claire had become a part of me. I couldn't abandon her now.

I returned my attention to the journal. "You say she's desperate, Dimity. You say she's deeply troubled. There must be a way to help her."

It could be dangerous.

"What's the alternative?" I asked. "To leave her in agony until another woman with my extremely rare qualifications just happens to visit Wyrdhurst?" I gripped the journal tightly. "I've felt Claire's longing, Dimity. I've experienced her grief. I can't walk away from her without at least trying to help."

I didn't think you would. Ah, well. If anyone can help Claire, you can, and there are ways to minimize the risks. Now that you're aware of her machinations, she won't be able to manipulate you so easily. She might even be willing to work with you. But you'll need something more. You'll need someone you can trust, to tether you to the world of the living.

I looked across the room, to the narrow iron bed I'd shared with Adam. I recalled the way he'd tucked the blankets in between us when I'd first awakened, and the humor he'd used to put me at ease. I'd been his for the taking up on the moors, but he hadn't taken me. Instead, he'd pushed me away, because it wasn't "right." Even now he watched me patiently, accepting without question what would have seemed to most men insane behavior.

"Would it be playing with fire to choose Adam?" I asked.

I think not. I've no doubt whatsoever that Claire has been trying to influence his behavior as well, but he's demonstrated admirable self-control when faced with temptation. He's clearly less vulnerable to her machinations than you are, and his invulnerability may help to protect you, now that you know what Claire's up to.

"Tell me what to do," I said.

Ask Claire to guide you. Something is amiss at Wyrdhurst. It must be put right or she'll never rest in peace. The handwriting stopped briefly. *Few people would put themselves at risk to help a suffering soul. I'm proud of you, Lori.*

Tears pricked my eyes even as I smiled. I brushed them away, closed the journal, and sat in silence, pondering how best to explain the inexplicable.

"Adam," I began. "Do you remember when I told you that I wasn't afraid of ghosts? . . ."

Two hours later, we sat across from each other at the pine table, eating bread and cheese and nursing mugs of tea. The blue journal lay beside the cutting board, and Reginald presided over the teapot. Adam had retrieved my flannel bunny from the wardrobe when he'd fetched the journal, but I'd been too dazed to notice at the time.

I cringed to think that I'd let Reg tumble to the floor while I cuddled the dashing Major Ted, but Reginald seemed unfazed by my disloyalty. He regarded me complacently, secure in the knowledge that no bear in uniform could ever take his place.

I kept my communion with Reginald to myself. I'd already given Adam enough food for years of thought, and though he'd accepted my improbable tale so far, I didn't want to push it.

"So," I said, "you'll come back to Wyrdhurst with me? You'll stay until I've found a way to help Claire?"

"Need you ask?" Adam slivered a curl of cheese and popped it into his mouth. "It's fascinating to think that Wyrdhurst is haunted after all, but by a ghost no one suspected."

"You must remind Claire of Edward," I said. "He's got dark hair and eyes, just like you. That's why I"—I caught myself—"why *she* finds you so attractive."

"Perhaps Josiah was right in keeping them apart," Adam observed.

"I'm not sure right and wrong come into it," I said. "Young love's a pretty powerful force. Bad things can happen when you get in its way. Do the names Romeo and Juliet ring a bell?"

"It was love, then," Adam said, "not simply adolescent urgings run amok?"

"It was for Claire," I replied. "I don't know about Edward."

"Why not?" Adam asked.

"He left, didn't he?" I shivered at the memory of Claire's voice speaking through me on the moors. "She pleaded with him to stay, but he left, and I don't know why."

"Perhaps his letters will tell us," said Adam.

"Will you help me find them?" I asked.

"Of course." Adam stared into the middle distance for a moment, then folded his arms and rested them on the table. "Thank you for taking me into your confidence, Lori. I swear to you that I'll never tell another living soul about Dimity and her journal."

"I know you won't." I poked his arm playfully. "I trust you, Adam."

He laughed a small, helpless laugh, as if my words had pained him. "Lori, there's something I must tell you. I—" He broke off, interrupted by the chirrup of the cell phone in my jacket pocket.

"Hold that thought," I told him, and hastened to answer the phone.

It was Guy, with reports on several fronts, each of which served to remind me that Nicole needed my help just as badly as young Claire.

Guy's men had found no evidence of an intruder on the terrace or in the tangled garden outside the library, and they were absolutely certain that no unauthorized vehicle had used the military track or the gated drive the night before.

"Whoever frightened Mrs. Hollander last night didn't come by car," Guy informed me. "Which leads me to Mr. Hollander and his alleged trip to Newcastle . . ."

Guy had been unable to locate Jared Hollander. He'd contacted owners of antique stores and auction houses in Newcastle, as well as private collectors of Victoriana, but no one had encountered Nicole's husband.

"By the same token," Guy went on, "my men haven't found his car. Six villagers saw him on Monday morning, driving toward the A696, which runs directly to Newcastle."

"He set out for Newcastle, then disappeared?" I grunted skeptically. "I'll bet he doubled back, hid the car out on the moors, and walked to Wyrdhurst. You can hide a lot on the moors. Adam and I found a crazy rock formation out there this morning, tucked away behind a hill."

"Yes," said Guy. "My men saw you."

A long minute passed, ample time for me to recall that I was speaking with a man who'd made heroic efforts to suppress his yearnings for a married woman.

"Guy," I cautioned. "It's not what you think."

"What I think is immaterial." His tone was arctic. "Do you plan to return to Wyrdhurst?"

"Yes," I said. "I wouldn't let Nicole spend the night there alone."

"I'm glad to hear it. I'll be in touch." Guy rang off without saying good-bye.

I folded the phone, turned, and stared at Adam. "That was Guy," I told him. "His men saw us, on the hill. He thinks we're slime."

"Does it matter what he thinks?" Adam came to stand before me. "The only one who matters is your husband." He took the cell phone from me, flipped it open, and handed it back. "Ring him. Now. I'll wait outside."

He gave me an encouraging wink before he left, but his parting glance was melancholy, as if he were just a little disappointed to know that the kiss had come from Claire and not from me.

Bill was pleased, not overjoyed, to hear from me.

"Can you hold a sec?" he asked, and before I could answer, he barked sternly, "Rob, if you don't give Daddy the rolling pin *at once,* Daddy's going to— Will, get your hands out of the marmalade *this minute* or I'll— Annelise!" His roar made my ear ring. "Could you give me a hand? Lori, I'll be right with you. . . . Boys! I said *right now.*"

There was a long pause during which I could hear the endearing, raucous sounds of my babies asserting their independence. Then Bill was back, apologizing for the interruption.

"Is everything okay?" I asked.

"Let's just say that you're not the only bullheaded member of the family," Bill replied.

"Stubbornness isn't such a bad trait," I temporized. "It may save the boys' lives someday."

"I'll bear that in mind while I'm wiping the marmalade handprints off the walls." Bill let out a whoosh, as thought he'd collapsed rather than settled into a convenient chair. "How about you? How's it going? Did the car arrive? And Dimity? She was incredibly anxious to join you, popped off her shelf three times, nearly clobbered Annelise twice. . . ."

The sound of his voice washed over me like honey, routing the dim shadows from my mind and rooting me firmly in a world I knew and loved.

"Lori," he said finally, "are you in some sort of trouble?"

I sank onto the armchair and smiled. "Not anymore."

CHAPTER

17

Adam and I returned to Wyrdhurst expecting fireworks, but nothing happened—no dizziness, no lightning bolts in my brain, and no irresistible urges to fling myself at someone other than my husband. Claire seemed to be keeping her distance, held in check, as Dimity had predicted, by Adam's anchoring presence and my own wariness.

We'd just finished piling Adam's overnight gear, Reginald, and the blue journal on the oak settle in the entrance hall when Mrs. Hatch emerged from the kitchen to inform us that Nicole was in the library.

"By herself?" I said, surprised.

"She insisted," Mrs. Hatch replied. "She's in a rare mood, that one. She said you were to go through when you get back. Would you please remind Mrs. Hollander that dinner will be on the table in forty minutes?"

I told her I would and hastened to the library, with Adam close on my heels.

Nicole was awake, fully dressed, and sitting on the sofa when we entered the room. She looked pale, but determined. When she saw us, she lifted her chin.

"I've been the most complete ninny," she announced. "I know very well that I didn't see a ghost last night."

Adam crossed to stand before the hearth, while I sat with Nicole on the sofa.

"What changed your mind?" I asked.

"As Dr. MacEwan quite rightly pointed out, ghosts don't exist." Nicole bit off each word cleanly before spitting it out. "Therefore, the thing I saw flying past the window must have been a human being." Her nostrils flared in anger. "Someone's trying to frighten me, Lori. On purpose. It's made me extremely cross."

The contrast between Nicole's little-girl vocabulary and her inflamed, adult emotion was so extreme that I couldn't restrain a short burst of involuntary laughter.

"Lori!" Nicole exclaimed, in high dudgeon.

I was immediately contrite. "I'm sorry. I didn't mean to laugh. It's great to see you up and punching. I'd rather you were angry than hysterical."

Nicole sniffed haughtily. "You won't see me hysterical again. I intend to go to Blackhope after dinner and tell those women exactly what I think of them."

Adam and I exchanged uncertain glances.

"Women?" I said.

"The chars," Nicole replied. "The women Jared dismissed. They've evidently decided to take their revenge on him by harassing me. It's unkind, unjust, and utterly uncalled-for."

"Are you sure about this?" I inquired.

"Am I sure that a flock of vindictive biddies has been pecking at me?" Nicole thought for a moment before admitting, "Not entirely. But who else could it be? Who else would play such cruel tricks on me?"

The opening was there, but I didn't take it. I couldn't bring myself to tell Nicole why her husband might be tempted to play cruel tricks on his wealthy, wide-eyed bride. But I could keep her from interfering with Guy's investigation.

"There's no need for you to go anywhere," I assured her. "Guy told me that he's aware of the situation, and that he's looking into it."

Nicole's nostrils flared alarmingly. "He told *you* and he didn't tell *me?*"

I quailed before her righteous indignation and decided, for Guy's sake, to mix a pinch of fiction in with the facts. "He called this morning, while you were, um, indisposed, and he's been really busy ever since. I'm sure he'll ring you the first chance he gets. He's worried sick about you, Nicole."

Nicole's blush, a tea-rose tint that gently bathed her fair complexion, filled me with envy. "I'd best leave it in his hands, then. Captain Manning's extremely competent."

A second lie popped into my head, a lie so wickedly untrue that I paused to examine it, to be sure it hadn't come from Claire. Once sure, I spoke.

"In fact," I said, darting a meaningful glance in Adam's direction, "Guy suggested that Adam stay with us, here at Wyrdhurst, until the culprits are caught. He told me he'd rest easier, knowing there's a man around to keep an eye on us."

Nicole lowered her eyelashes and leaned close to me. "Captain Manning doesn't suspect . . . ?"

I shook my head. "He never did."

"I'm glad." Nicole gave my arm a gentle squeeze before addressing Adam. "Thank you so much for watching over us, Mr. Chase. I'll have Mrs. Hatch prepare the blue room for you. You'll dine with us, I hope?"

"I'd be honored," he said. "I'd be even more honored if you'd call me Adam. And, by the way, Mrs. Hatch asked us to remind you that dinner will be served in"—he consulted the ebony clock—"thirty minutes."

"Thank you . . . Adam. And you must call me Nicole. I'm sure my husband won't mind." Nicole ducked her head and went on, with a slightly sheepish grin. "It seems that I shan't be visiting my wrath upon Blackhope after dinner. How shall we spend the evening? Charades? Cards?"

A cool breeze chilled the back of my neck and I turned in its direction. My gaze met Josiah's briefly before flitting to the notes on the oak table.

"Nicole," I said, "with your permission, I'd like to find out where the secret staircase goes."

Nicole was up for a bit of exploration, especially after I suggested that the staircase might lead us to Edith Ann Malson's books, and Edward's letters. After dining on delectable roast pheasant and sugary damson pie, we went our separate ways to prepare for the evening's expedition.

I took the advice I'd given my companions and bundled up against the staircase's bitter chill. I changed into tweed trousers and pulled a wool sweater over a turtleneck for added warmth. It wasn't until I reached for my flashlight that I felt a strange quiver of foreboding and realized that it wasn't my own.

I went to the bedside table, kissed the three beloved faces in the framed photograph, fondled Reginald's pink flannel ears, and laid my hand on the blue journal.

"I'm here to help you, Claire," I said to the empty air. "I won't let anything—or anyone—hurt you."

Something touched my mind, gentle as a butterfly's wing, and I knew that Claire was with me once again. It was an unnerving sensation but less frightening than I'd expected it to be, as if Claire had decided that she'd accomplish more through teamwork than through stealth. Even so, I was relieved when Adam called through my door, to find out if I was ready.

"She's back," I said, joining him in the corridor.

"I thought she might be. I heard an odd note in your voice when you asked Nicole about the secret staircase."

"You think Claire planted the idea?" I touched a finger to my temple. "Why not? She led me to Edward's notes. Now she wants to guide me to his letters."

"How are you feeling?" Adam asked.

"A little strange, but basically okay. It helps to know what's happening." I looked up at him. "Stay close, will you? You have my husband's blessing."

Adam shook his head. "Your husband is a most unusual man."

"I know," I said, with a wry smile. "Aunt Dimity had a hand in his upbringing."

Nicole was waiting for us in the library, sensibly but beautifully clad in black wool trousers and a lush bronze velvet tunic. As we came through the study doors, she held up two flashlights and a camping lantern.

"There's no electricity laid on above the second story," she explained, "so I thought a bright light might be useful. Here's a torch for you, Adam." She waved her own flashlight in the air. "It's rather exciting, isn't it? Like exploring King Tut's tomb. I haven't been able to open the bookcase, though. Do you remember how it happened, Lori?"

I closed my eyes and let my mind grow quiet. Suddenly, without conscious effort, I saw myself from above, going through the same motions I'd gone through the first time the hidden door had opened. It was like watching a little film shown on my eyelids. By the time the credits rolled, I knew what to do. If I hadn't been so rattled by my frightening experience on the staircase, I would have remembered it much sooner.

I took *Shuttleworth's Birds* from the oak table, put it back on the shelf where I'd found it, and pulled it out again. A moment later, the bookshelf swung smoothly and silently into the room.

"How strange." Nicole approached the door, bent low, then straightened, rubbing her thumb against her index finger. "The hinges have been oiled recently. Someone's been using this staircase." Her mouth compressed into a thin line. "Jared's probably known about it all along. It would be just like him to keep it from me. He's always going on at me about his need for privacy."

"Maybe he meant to surprise you," Adam suggested.

"He's going to receive a few surprises when he comes home," Nicole said grimly. "I'll lead the way," she added. "Adam, you take up the rear. If Lori stumbles, you're to catch her."

"I'm not going to stumble," I grumbled.

"Nevertheless . . ." said Nicole, and we entered the staircase in the order she'd dictated.

My companions seemed oblivious to the chill, but I felt as if I'd stepped into a Deepfreeze. I'd just pulled my icy hands up into the sleeves of my wool sweater when Nicole came to an abrupt halt.

"Look." She pointed to two narrow beams of light that pierced the darkness from left to right. "Someone's drilled two tiny little holes in the wall."

"The glowing eyes," I whispered. A cold hand seemed to trail down my spine. "Josiah's portrait. Adam, check his eyes."

Adam retreated to the library. A moment later the twin beams vanished briefly, then reappeared.

"You're right, Lori," Adam said as he rejoined us. "There's a pinhole in each of the portrait's eyes. They're small, but large enough, I'll wager, to give someone inside the staircase a good view of the library."

As Nicole leaned forward to peer through the peepholes, a low-pitched, malevolent chuckle floated through the darkness, echoing eerily from the cold stone walls. I stiffened and Nicole leapt back with a shriek. As soon as she stepped away from the peepholes, the laughter faded.

"What was *that?*" she gasped.

Adam stepped past me, shining his light on the ceiling, the steps, and the walls, until its beam came to rest on a small black box directly opposite the peepholes, affixed to the wall with duct tape. He waved his hand in front of the box and the laughter sounded again.

"I'm no expert," he said, "but I think we've found a tape recorder wired to a motion detector. When you stepped in front of it, Nicole, you set off the recording." He drew his flashlight through the air, and the maniacal chuckle resumed.

Nicole's sharp intake of breath cut through the menacing laughter.

"I'll have Jared's head," she proclaimed. "How *dare* he? Hiding his private staircase from me is bad enough, but trying to keep people from using it by scaring them out of their wits is . . . is . . . *unconscionable.*"

With an angry snarl, she wrenched the black box from the wall and flung it down the staircase, narrowly missing my head.

"We don't know that Jared rigged the box," Adam pointed out. "We don't even know if he uses the staircase."

"Don't we?" Nicole snapped. "Unless I'm very much mistaken, these stairs lead directly to his bedroom. It used to be Josiah's room, you know. I thought that's why Jared wanted it—so he could play at being lord of the manor—but perhaps he had other reasons."

She charged ahead, so furious that I could almost see steam shooting from her ears. I smiled inwardly, noting for the first time the strong resemblance between my young friend and her hard-nosed uncle Dickie.

I was more relieved than angered by the discovery of the black box, glad to know that the mysterious, menacing laughter had a terrestrial source. Still, I felt uneasy on the staircase.

"You're awfully quiet." As Adam came closer, his hand brushed mine. "Good Lord," he muttered, "you're freezing."

"Aren't you?" I asked.

"No," he replied. "I've been wondering why you told us to dress warmly."

"It must be Claire." I turned to look at the peepholes and felt the shadow of a shudder of revulsion, as if Claire were looking through my eyes at something that repulsed her.

Adam chafed my hand. "What is it, Lori? Talk to me."

"I don't know who planted the black box," I said, "but I'm pretty sure that Josiah Byrd drilled those holes. I think he used them to spy on his daughter."

"He must have been mad," said Adam.

"Maybe he was. Maybe that's why Claire hates this place." I turned to him. "She truly hates it. That's why I'm so cold, why I passed out the last time I was here. She couldn't stand the thought of going up these stairs. But she's stronger now, more resolute. I think she—"

I broke off, startled, and our heads swung upward as we heard a thud, a crash, and Nicole's voice ringing triumphant from above:

"I knew it!"

CHAPTER

18

Jared's bedroom reminded me of a Victorian bordello, replete with ostrich feathers, red-shaded lamps, and highly detailed oil paintings of flimsily clad youths and maidens reposing languorously amid Roman ruins.

A white marble statue of two wrestlers lay in pieces at Nicole's feet. She'd knocked it from its plinth when she'd burst into the room, but she showed no sign whatsoever of remorse. She stood, tight-lipped and silently seething, while Adam and I took in the room's unusual decor.

"Come along." She spun on her heel and shooed us back onto the secret-staircase landing just outside the room. "We'll find no children's books here."

I was forced to agree. I suspected that the kind of books we'd find in Jared's bedroom weren't the kind of books most people kept in nurseries.

"Jared camouflaged the entrance to the staircase with wallpaper," she continued, slamming the door shut behind her. "I don't know why he bothered. I've scarcely set foot in his bedroom since we took possession of Wyrdhurst."

"It must be that privacy thing of his," I put in lamely.

"Oh, he'll have all the privacy he wants from now on." Nicole's eyes glittered so dangerously that I almost felt sorry for her husband.

Beyond the landing, the staircase twisted upward in a narrow corkscrew spiral. The steps were so steep and shallow that I felt as if I were climbing a ladder. Nicole and I were soon huffing, but Adam seemed untroubled by the climb. I called to mind his athlete's build and the ease with which he'd rescued Reginald from the crash site, and concluded that he must be part mountain goat.

"I think we're in the west tower," Nicole informed us between gasps. "It's used for storage. I wonder if Miss Malson's books—Wait . . . I think we've reached the top."

Adam and I crowded together as the beam from Nicole's flashlight illuminated a second landing and a Gothic-arched, heavy wooden door.

"If it's locked," Nicole declared, "I shall scream."

"It's not locked," I said, under my breath. "Not anymore." With those words came an awareness that I was no longer shivering. The deep chill had left my body. The queer flutter of butterfly wings had vanished, too.

Claire was gone. It was as if she'd brought me to a threshold she couldn't bring herself to cross. She'd unlocked the door, but she needed me to take the final step.

I squeezed past Nicole, put my shoulder to the door, and shoved, to no effect. Adam joined me and together we got

the stingy hinges to give, under protest, splintering the silence with a shrill, nerve-pinching squeal. Flashlights thrust
before us, we edged cautiously into the room beyond the
Gothic doorway.

The room was round, with white-plastered walls and a
floor laid with wide, rough-hewn planks. The ceiling was low
and divided by beams in a pattern like spokes in a wheel. Six
wavy-paned windows pierced the walls, each little more
than an arrow slit, and the only door was the one we'd used,
coming in from the hidden staircase.

We stood apart as Nicole joined us, but no one said a
word. Our bright beams striped the darkness, crossing and
parting like klieg lights as we picked out the room's simple
furnishings: a thin gray mattress on a bed as narrow as
Adam's; an iron washstand with a plain white ewer and basin;
a blanket chest; an unpainted deal table; a chest-high cupboard; a simple grate set in a white-plastered chimney
breast. A wooden chair sat near the grate. Beside the chair
stood an embroidery frame on a three-legged wooden stand.

"It's not a nursery," Nicole observed sagely. "I don't know
what it is." She walked past us, placed her lantern on the table,
and peered out of the nearest window. "We're in the west
tower," she confirmed, "but this room isn't marked in the
floor plans. What made you think that Edward's letters might
be in this peculiar little room?"

I looked from the embroidery frame to the thin gray
mattress and felt a sick sensation in the pit of my stomach.
"Just a hunch," I said. "I think Claire may have . . . spent time
up here."

Nicole turned away from the window. "She probably
came up here for the view. Imagine Jared keeping this to

himself." She laughed, a small, bitter laugh. "Who was it who said that a wife's always the last to know?"

"An unmarried idiot," I stated firmly. "Nicole, Jared may or may not know about the staircase, but he's never been up here. Look at the floor. It's furred with dust, and the only footprints are ours. No one's been up here in a long, long time."

Nicole lit the camping lantern and the room was flooded with light.

"I suppose you're right." She looked askance at our footprints before adding snidely, "I doubt Jared's strong enough to open the door on his own."

I was about to comment on the imprudence of hanging a man before he was tried and convicted when Adam spoke.

"Ladies," he said, kneeling before the wooden cupboard, "I think I've found what you've been looking for."

He swung the cupboard's doors wide to reveal row after row of brightly colored books. The rainbow bindings stood out in the dust-gray room as vividly as a cardinal on a snowy bough.

I recognized some of them on sight: Elizabeth Baumgartner's fairy books, Hannah Manderley's collection of fables, and, filling the bottom shelf from side to side, a complete set of Edith Ann Malson.

"Adam," I said, "you're my hero."

Adam cleared the bottom shelf in a trice and piled the books on the table. We flipped through the pages with feverish speed, ignoring Monmouth Mouse, Romney Rat, and the rest of Edith Ann's charming rodents, intent only on finding the letters her books had concealed.

We found nothing.

"Keep looking," I said, and the real search began.

We fanned through every book in the cupboard, looked under the mattress, into the ewer, and inside the blanket chest. Adam stood on the chair and ran his hands along the rafters while Nicole rapped walls and I crawled on my hands and knees, hoping to find a loose floorboard. Adam even removed the grate and stuck his arm up the flue, but still we found no trace of the letters. The blanket chest held nothing but a sewing basket, the ewer nothing but dust, and there was nothing up the flue but spiderwebs.

With a disconsolate sigh, Nicole sank onto the blanket chest, and Adam perched on the edge of the bed, his head in his hands. I stood over the table, staring down at Edith Ann Malson's books, knowing that Claire was depending on me to ferret out her hiding place.

"What a pity." Nicole brushed cobwebs from her velvet tunic. "We must have misinterpreted Edward's note."

"Or someone else found the letters already," Adam murmured.

"No," I said. "She was afraid that someone would find the letters. That's why she hid them." I gave Nicole a sideways glance. "What's in the sewing basket?"

"The usual items." She lifted the wicker basket from the chest and removed the lid. "Needles, reels of silk, thimbles, scissors . . . It's not even lined with cloth. If it were, Claire might have sewn the letters into the—"

"That's it!" I snapped my fingers. "Adam, get up." I reached the bed in two loping strides, heaved the mattress up on edge, and ran my fingers along the seams until I found an irregularity in the stitching. "Nicole," I said, "give me the scissors."

The tiny embroidery scissors were sharp enough to slit the seam from end to end. I slipped a hand inside the mattress and caught my breath as my fingertips touched paper. I looked from Nicole's face to Adam's, then laughed in sheer exultation.

"They're here," I crowed. "We've found them!"

CHAPTER

19

We sat up all night in the library, bolstered by endless pots of tea and plates full of Claire's Lace, first arranging the letters in chronological order, then reading them aloud, one by one.

Nicole and I sat on the sofa, Adam in the armchair nearest the fire. The letters lay on a low table between us, one hundred and forty-four creased and frail sheets, one for nearly every week that Edward Frederick Cresswell had served his king and country in the Great European War.

We soon left the reading to Adam, in part because he understood the war's language and events and could explain them to us, but mainly because he was a man, reading a man's words.

Emotions flickered like firelight across his face as he deciphered the smudged pencilings, as if he saw what Edward saw, felt what Edward felt, crouched beside him in the clinging mud as shells shrieked overhead, caught death's stench in the softest summer breeze, watched friends reduced to ragged lumps of flesh.

An early letter, sent from training camp in October 1914, told us why Edward had made the decision to leave Claire.

> *I know you don't agree with my decision to join up, but I can think of no other way to win your father's approval. I haven't the great fortune or the title he so ardently desires for you, but I have courage, strength, and the resolve to use them. Providence has given me a chance to prove myself worthy of you. Oxford can wait. My love for you cannot.*
>
> *Some men have embarked upon this great adventure for God and England. I've done it for you alone. When I return a hero, your father will be forced to give us his blessing.*
>
> *My greatest fear is that I'll miss the shooting match. They're saying it will all be over by Christmas. . . .*

The war wasn't over by Christmas. Edward was shipped to France on April 3, 1915, and sent up to the firing line ten days later. A mud-stained note headed "In the Trenches— Flanders" answered several more questions, including one we hadn't thought to ask.

> *Sorry about the awful scrawl, but if you could see my writing table, you'd understand. It's a broken bit*

*of duckboard, which is propped on my knees, which
are propped on my boots, which are in turn planted
in eight inches of muck. If I stay still long enough, I
may sprout roots and branches.*

*I've sent you a small gift, purchased in London
while awaiting final orders. Although he's a Major,
and I a mere Second Lieutenant, I hope he'll remind
you of your own dear Teddy, who misses you desper-
ately.*

"Good heavens," Nicole exclaimed. "I believe Edward's
speaking of Major Ted."

"I think you're right," I said. "Claire's pet name for Edward must have been Teddy."

"But you've always called Major Ted 'Teddy.'" Nicole
looked at me strangely. "It's as if you knew his proper name
all along."

I knew who'd planted Major Ted's proper name in my
mind, but I couldn't explain it to Nicole. For the time being,
she needed to believe that the Wyrdhurst ghost was a myth
concocted by the villagers. The truth would only frighten
and confuse her.

Adam's thoughts evidently ran parallel to my own, because he tossed out a plausible explanation.

"It's a common enough name for a teddy bear," he said. "I
imagine that's why he sent Claire a bear. It allowed her to
speak his name without alerting her father." He bent his head
over the letter, adding, "I think you'll find this next bit even
more interesting."

> *When I think of how I resented Mother for forcing me to spend the summer hols with Uncle Clive, I can only laugh. If she hadn't insisted, I might never have discovered the moors' indelible beauty—or yours. God bless her!*
>
> *And God bless Uncle Clive. He'll pass my gift off as his own, and deliver my letters in the usual manner. Who'd have thought we'd owe so much to Miss Malson's mouse?*

"Clive," I said slowly. The name rang a distant bell, but I couldn't quite place it.

Adam could. "Clive Eccles Aynsworth," he said. "He was the schoolmaster in Blackhope. There's a plaque in the church commemorating his death."

"Clive Aynsworth catalogued Great-grandfather's library," Nicole interjected. She turned to me. "Didn't you see his name on the back of the ledger?"

"I didn't spend much time on the ledger," I confessed.

"Clive Aynsworth was the perfect go-between," Adam mused aloud. "As a cataloguer, he had easy access to Wyrdhurst and could carry books back and forth without drawing attention to himself."

I called to mind the story Guy had told me beside the brush pile in Blackhope. "Josiah must have found out what he was doing, and decided to put a stop to it."

"A full stop," Adam added.

Nicole didn't know what we were talking about. She'd never heard of the mysterious fire that had killed Clive

Aynsworth. When I explained the villagers' suspicions, she surprised me by accepting the grim tale as something well within the realm of possibility.

"Josiah's temper was legendary," she said. "He was known for flying into ungovernable rages. If he discovered what Clive Aynsworth was up to, he might well have taken matters into his own hands." She gazed at Josiah's portrait knowingly. "We don't call him the old devil for nothing."

The ebony clock chimed midnight, Adam added coal to the fire, and Nicole rang for more tea and cookies. No one mentioned turning in for the night. Our questions seemed less important now than Edward's ongoing journey. I wasn't sure about the others, but I felt compelled to accompany him until he'd reached his final destination.

A note of insouciance had brightened his first reports from the front. Six weeks later, the brightness had vanished.

> *Most machines take disparate bits and build them into something useful. The war machine takes something useful—a man—and smashes him into bloody bits.*
>
> *I've seen things I can never tell to you, but that's not the horror. The horror is that I no longer think them horrible. The stench, the filth, the blood, the rotting corpses of men better and braver by far than myself, all have become as familiar to me as the heather on the hills.*
>
> *There are no heroes here. Only the dead, and those who soon shall be.*

He survived the advent of poisoned gas in the Second Battle of Ypres, and carried on unscathed through the charnel house of the Somme, only to be wounded by a sniper during a period of relative calm. The wound was a minor shoulder graze, not the coveted "blighty" that would send a soldier home, but the time he spent recuperating in rest camp seemed to restore to him a measure of serenity.

> They've fed us on roast beef and Yorkshire pudding—my favorite, as you know—and let us sit quietly in the sun. We all pretend it's thunder rumbling in the distance, instead of cannon.
> I suppose I'm a real soldier at last, blooded but unbowed, able to snatch poetry from the tedium and the terror. An artillery barrage may be a nightmare, but it can be a beautiful nightmare, and war can be exhilarating beyond anything I'd imagined.

He returned to England several times on leave, but it wasn't until June 1917 that he and Claire were able to meet face to face.

> I hope now to get leave about June 25th. If the trains are running, I'll be at the Ring on Thursday, when your father's in Newcastle. Come to me, heart's dearest.

I closed my eyes and saw once again the moors mantled with supple green grasses. I met Adam's gaze and felt desire stir within me, but knew that it wasn't my own. The passion I'd felt when I'd seen the Devil's Ring had been the passion of young lovers tasting heaven after nearly three years in hell.

When Edward returned to the front, he wrote:

> *Your Lace made it all the way without a crumble.*
> *I've shared it out among the men, who think it the*
> *sweetest confection on earth. They're wrong, of*
> *course—you are.*
>
> *It all seems like a dream, the grass and the heather*
> *and the great gray stones—a perfect paradise with*
> *you as the presiding angel. I feared that I had*
> *changed beyond all knowing, but you knew me, you*
> *have always known me, and you helped me to know*
> *myself once more.*
>
> *We've broken all of your father's rules, but I can't*
> *believe we've put our souls in danger. Our hearts*
> *were pure when we entered the Ring and will re-*
> *main so, come what may.*
>
> *This day was ours to hold fast in our hearts. I*
> *hope and pray there will be many more, but if there*
> *aren't, this day, at least, was ours.*

"He's talking about the Devil's Ring," Nicole said. "Uncle Dickie took me there once. He tried to frighten me with a horrible old legend."

"Those who enter the Ring must be pure of heart or risk losing their immortal souls to the devil." Adam's dark eyes sought and held mine. "I agree with Edward. He and Claire had nothing to fear from the devil. If ever hearts were pure, theirs were."

I gave a small nod and he replied with a half-regretful smile. We needn't fear for our souls, he was saying. Our embrace was a gift to Claire.

"You speak as if you know them," Nicole observed.

"I feel as if I do," said Adam. "Don't you?"

"I suppose so," Nicole conceded. "Claire, more than Edward. She was young and lonely and . . . and afraid. For Edward, I mean." Her expression became solemn, as if she'd realized that Claire's problems weren't so different from her own. "Please, Adam, go on reading."

Adam bent to his task.

In July 1917, Edward and a fellow subaltern called Mitchell were given a temporary assignment at Corps Headquarters.

> We're well out of the danger zone, billeted in a rather grand château. With another push impending, it's a perfect zoo, but we bathe daily, sleep in beds, and have sugar for our tea, so we've no call to complain.

The next letter, written two days later, proved intriguing.

> Mitchell and I were cycling past the château's walled garden this morning when a stray shell—one of ours, from the practice range—landed not a hundred yards from us. We dove for Mother Earth, were pelted with the usual debris—and something else, something wonderful.

The garden coughed up buried treasure! We could scarcely believe our eyes. It was as if a gift had fallen from heaven, and we quickly decided it would be impious to reject the deity's offering.

You'll think me reprehensible, my darling, but the château's owner is dead, his sole heir was killed at Verdun, and I'm dashed if I'll turn it over to "the proper authorities." They've long since taken from me more than their fair share.

I'm posting my portion home to you, as a constant reminder of the vows we'll take when next we meet, regardless of your father's disapproval.

The hoped-for meeting never came, and the vows were never spoken. A newspaper clipping, folded in among the letters, gave notice that on Saturday, September 8, 1917, three years after he'd enlisted, Edward Frederick Cresswell was killed in action, in the Third Battle of Ypres, known to the soldiers who fought there as Passchendaele.

He'd just turned twenty-one.

"Poor Claire," Nicole said softly. "She must have died of a broken heart."

The last letter of all was written in a careful, copybook script quite different from Edward's scrawl.

Dear Miss Byrd,

Please pardon me for writing, but I feel as if I know you. Ted talked about you always, and he showed your picture round every chance he got. He was a fine man, and I'm proud to have served with him. I know you'll miss him sorely, but I hope you'll take some comfort knowing that his men thought highly of him and that he's resting now in a Better Place.

Yours truly,
2nd Lieutenant P. Mitchell

The first light of dawn was seeping into the room when Adam finished Lieutenant Mitchell's letter. His voice was hoarse, his face drawn, as if the night's journey had exhausted him. He placed the last frail sheet beside the newspaper clipping, rose from his chair, and crossed to the brass telescope, where he stood staring out across the gray and empty moors.

I listened to the ticking of the ebony clock, filled with a sense of numbing defeat. Edward had survived so much and for so long that he'd come to seem invincible. I couldn't quite believe that he was dead.

"Passchendaele." Adam spoke with his back to us, in a hollow, faraway voice. "A lowland village surrounded by bogs drained by a system of dikes and canals. Artillery barrages destroyed the drainage system, and when the rains came, the bogs were reborn.

"Farm fields became sucking quagmires that swallowed horses whole. Wounded men pitched forward into the mud and drowned. The dead sank without a trace. More than forty thousand soldiers vanished in the insatiable sea of mud. Local farmers still harvest their bones."

I exchanged a worried glance with Nicole and went to stand at Adam's side. His eyes were glazed, unblinking, as if he were in a trance, and I felt a stab of guilt for leaving so much of the reading to him. It had been hard enough to listen to Edward's words. To read them, in the boy's own hand, on paper stained with battlefield filth, must have been wrenching.

"He has no grave," Adam murmured. "Josiah has a mausoleum, but Edward has no grave."

Adam knew better than I that Flanders was littered with military cemeteries, but it wasn't the time or the place to remind him.

"He had Claire's love," I said softly. "Surely that was enough." I twined my arm in his. "It's been a long night. I think we could all do with a little sleep."

He raised a hand to rub his tired eyes. "Yes. We'll talk more in the morning."

"It's morning already," I said, but Adam made no reply.

He turned and left the room, moving like a sleepwalker, with Nicole and me trailing after him, each of us grieving in silence for a young man we'd never known and the young woman who'd loved him.

CHAPTER

20

I stayed up longer than I'd intended, curled on the fainting couch in my flannel nightie, savoring the fire's warmth and telling Aunt Dimity about the staircase, the tower room, and Edward. When I finished, her first response was one of almost comic indignation.

I simply cannot abide ghost impersonators. Wyrdhurst is troubled enough without adding amateur apparitions to the mix. Apart from that, they've no sense of subtlety. The tape-recorded laughter wouldn't have frightened you for more than two minutes if you hadn't been under Claire's influence. I can't imagine why any self-respecting faker would use such a silly, childish toy.

"Jared might have rigged the black box to serve as an alarm," I suggested. "The laughter would confuse an intruder and warn Jared that someone was on his staircase."

You're convinced that Jared's responsible, then?

"He's the most likely suspect," I replied. "He has the motive and, as far as I know, the opportunity."

Don't you find it odd that he never entered the tower room?

"I'm pretty sure that the door to the tower room was locked until last night," I said, "when Claire unlocked it for me."

Yet she couldn't enter the room herself. I have a bad feeling about that place, Lori.

I heard a soft tap at the door, set the journal aside, and called out, "Come in."

Adam stepped into the room. "I saw the light under your door," he said. "Mind if I join you?"

"Not at all." I swung my legs to the floor, to make room for him on the fainting couch.

He closed the door behind him. He was still wearing the clothes he'd worn all night, and he looked dog-tired, as if he hadn't slept in weeks.

As he sank onto the couch I said, "I know this'll sound ridiculous, coming from me, but you really should be in bed."

"I know." His voice was rough with fatigue. "It's absurd, isn't it? I'm exhausted, but I can't sleep."

"It's my fault," I said. "I shouldn't have left all of the reading to you. I know how deeply you sympathize with the soldiers who—"

"Please, Lori," he broke in. "Please don't apologize to me. I don't think I could bear it." He sat with his elbows on his knees, staring at the floor. "Besides, it's not the letters, it's that room, that awful room. I can't get it out of my mind."

"Dimity has a bad feeling about it," I told him.

"So do I." He looked over his shoulder at the barred windows. "It's all of a piece—the bars, the telescope, the peepholes, Claire's fears. . . . I keep thinking about the embroidery frame and that pathetic collection of children's books." He turned his red-rimmed eyes toward me. "Shall I tell you why the room was built?"

I nodded reluctantly. I didn't really want to hear his answer.

"Josiah treated his daughter like a prisoner," Adam said. "I think he finally built a prison for her."

I envisioned the isolated, barren room, with its heavy door and slender windows, but shook my head.

"We're not talking about the Middle Ages," I protested. "Josiah wasn't a feudal lord. He couldn't snap his fingers and make people vanish."

"Couldn't he?" Adam's gaze intensified. "Wyrdhurst is a world unto itself, Lori, and Josiah built it. He created the staircase and the tower room, and he made sure that he alone had access to both. Do you think he excluded them from the floor plans by accident?"

"But someone would notice that Claire was missing," I insisted. "Someone would . . ." A sick feeling of dread welled up inside of me. "Clive Aynsworth. He must have found the hidden door in the library and figured out what Josiah was up to. *That's* why Josiah killed him—to prevent him from telling people that Claire was in the tower."

Adam motioned toward the windows. "Josiah tried putting bars on her bedroom windows, but they didn't do the trick. I believe he shut her up in the tower to keep her from running away."

"He couldn't keep her there forever," I said.

"Not forever." Adam gave a shuddering sigh. "Just until Edward was dead."

A coal fell on the fire, sending up a shower of sparks. Beyond the windows, the sun had risen on another crisp autumn day. How often had Claire looked out from her cell, I wondered, remembering sunny mornings on the moors?

"He must have been insane," I murmured.

"There was a time," said Adam, "when we would have called him evil." He ran a hand through his hair. "I'm sorry. I shouldn't have dropped this on you, not at this hour, not after last night."

"I'm glad you did." I went to the bedside table and brought Major Ted to Adam. "Here. Take Teddy with you. He'll stand guard over your dreams."

"No nightmares shall pass?" Adam smiled, took the bear, and stood. "Thank you, Lori, for—"

"Don't be silly," I scolded. "Now go to bed."

When he'd gone, I took up the blue journal. The handwriting began the moment I turned the first page.

Adam seems deeply disturbed.

"He's had a tough night," I reminded her. "He's studied the First World War. He knows what Edward went through and"—I hesitated—"and I suppose he feels close to Claire. She chose him to stand in for Edward. In a sense, he's held her in his arms."

He has feelings for you as well, Lori.

"I know." I hadn't missed the half-regretful smile or the shadow of sadness in his eyes, and I couldn't deny a certain sadness of my own. Adam and I had been through a lot together, in a very short period of time. It would have been inhuman to feel nothing.

It seems almost inevitable, given the circumstances.

"Yes." Dimity had touched a tender place and I shied away from her probing. "Dimity, Adam believes that Josiah imprisoned Claire in the tower room. Do you think he's right?"

I do. It explains so much. Still, I feel certain that something else happened in that room, something terrible, more terrible than imprisonment, more terrible even than Edward's death.

I blanched as a horrifying possibility presented itself. "Do you think Josiah *murdered* Claire?"

I don't know. I only know that Claire's tormented by unfinished business and unhealed wounds. This house is haunted by its past, Lori.

I shrugged helplessly. "I can't change the past."

But you can change the present. Claire led you to Edward's letters for a reason.

I thought for a moment. "The treasure," I said finally. "She wants me to find the treasure Edward sent to her."

She wants you to piece the puzzle together properly, the way it should have been done so many years ago. Only then will she be able to rest in peace.

Now follow your own advice, my dear, and go to bed. You'll need your wits about you to help Claire reach her final destination.

Nicole was the first to broach the intriguing subject that had been justifiably overshadowed by Edward's death.

We'd gathered in the dining room for a hearty English breakfast served by Hatch at the unconventional hour of two o'clock in the afternoon. Seven hours of sleep had restored Nicole's peace of mind, but Adam still looked troubled. He ate in silence while Nicole and I discussed the tantalizing hint Edward had dropped in his final letter to Claire.

Nicole kicked the conversation off by announcing that she'd telephoned Uncle Dickie, to tell him of the night's adventure, and discovered that he knew nothing about the hidden staircase or the tower room. What's more, he'd never heard of Edward Cresswell or the treasure that had supposedly come into Claire's possession in 1917.

"I do wish Edward had been more specific about the *kind* of thing he'd sent," Nicole complained, scooping marmalade from a pretty porcelain jam pot.

"What would the owner of a French château bury in his garden?" I asked.

"Jewelry," Nicole answered promptly. "That's what I'd bury if the Scots threatened to invade Northumberland." She giggled girlishly, glimpsed Adam's solemn face, and straightened her own. "Uncle Dickie wondered if Claire actually received the treasure."

"I don't see why not," I said. "Clive Aynsworth was a faithful courier. He wouldn't have kept back a package meant for Claire, particularly since she already knew it was coming." I put my teacup down abruptly as a jarring thought struck home. "It must have been the last package he delivered."

"Why is that?" Nicole asked.

Adam spoke for the first time. "If you'll examine the memorial tablet in the church, you'll see that Clive Aynsworth died less than a month after Edward. Lori's probably right. The treasure was the last thing Mr. Aynsworth brought to Claire."

"How sad." Nicole allowed a decent interval to pass before returning to a subject that had evidently seized her imagination. "Claire must have hidden the treasure, just as she did the letters, to keep Josiah from confiscating it."

"She didn't hide it in the tower room," I stated flatly. "If she had, we'd've found it last night."

"Where else could it be?" Nicole paused to contemplate a marmalade-slathered triangle of toast. "Claire last saw Edward at the Devil's Ring. Do you suppose she might have buried the treasure there?" She turned to Adam. "What do you say, Adam? Shall we mount an expedition?"

Adam blinked slowly, as if Nicole had awakened him from a deep sleep. "Not today," he said softly. "It'll be dark by the time we get there."

Nicole grimaced. "I don't fancy visiting the Devil's Ring at night. We'll go tomorrow, if the weather's fine." She nodded, satisfied, and continued eating.

"I think we should search the rooms on the third floor," I proposed, "the ones you haven't renovated yet."

"Really?" Nicole's good cheer vanished abruptly. "You know, I haven't been up to the third floor since we took possession of Wyrdhurst. The . . . the noises I've heard, the footsteps, the creaks—they always seem to come from up there."

"Then it's high time someone had a look around," I told her. "You said yourself that humans are behind all of this ghost nonsense. Let's see if we can find proof—and the treasure."

"Are you acting on another hunch?" Nicole inquired.

"No," I admitted. Claire hadn't made herself known to me since she'd left me at the tower room. I suspected that she, like Adam, needed time to recover from our difficult journey into the past. "I just think we ought to cover all of the bases. We can search the third-floor rooms today and the Devil's Ring tomorrow."

"Well . . ." Nicole took a deep breath and straightened her shoulders. "If you're up to it, I'm game. What about you, Adam?"

"Adam needs a few more hours of sleep," I said.

He looked at me gratefully. "You may be right, Lori, but it's not a wise idea." He lowered his long lashes, a faint smile tugging at his lips. "Captain Manning would accuse me of dereliction of duty."

I gave him a covert glare. I'd nursed a faint hope that Nicole would forget the whopper I'd told to explain Adam's presence at Wyrdhurst, but I should have known better. When it came to Captain Manning, Nicole had a mind like a steel trap.

"I'm glad you take your assignment seriously, Adam, but I'm sure G——Captain Manning won't mind us being on our own during the day. It's only at night that strange things happen." She patted Adam's hand. "You go back to your room and have a nice lie-down. If Lori and I find anything, you'll be the first to know."

As I swallowed a last bite of smoked salmon, it occurred to me that I hadn't heard from Guy since he'd reached me by telephone at the fishing hut. I wondered briefly if he'd managed to locate Nicole's missing husband or identify the culprit who'd opened the gate to the military track. On the whole, however, I welcomed his silence. I wasn't looking forward to his reaction when Nicole thanked him for sending Adam to watch over us.

"It's rather spooky, isn't it?" Nicole whispered.

The east-wing corridor lay before us, as surreal as the deck of a drowned ocean liner. Wyrdhurst's elaborate Victorian decor ended abruptly at the third floor. Gone were the polished tables, the velvet hangings, the gilt-framed oils. Instead, ragged ribbons of faded wallpaper drooped from the walls, tarnished sconces hung askew, and a fine layer of dust covered everything in a ghostly gray shroud.

The silence was so profound that we crept along like truant children fearing discovery. I wore my cat-burglar outfit, Nicole a russet sweater and tweed trousers, and we both carried flashlights.

"I'm sorry it's so filthy," Nicole went on. "The cleaners come up here only once a month."

"I don't mind," I whispered back. "It gives the place a certain *je ne sais quoi.*"

Nicole's giggle echoed eerily from the peeling walls.

"Lori," she said suddenly. Her normal tone of voice rang out like a shout. "Someone's been here before us."

"I know," I said. "Hatch and those two men you sent up to the east tower have been here before us."

"But . . . why would they stop at every room?"

She directed her flashlight along the floor and I saw on the threadbare runner row after row of blurred footprints leading to and from every door along the corridor.

"Mrs. Hatch?" I suggested.

"She never comes up here, and the cleaners haven't been for three weeks." Nicole took her lower lip between her teeth. "We should fetch Adam. Better yet, we should ring Guy. Guy will know what to do."

"You're being a ninny again." I had no intention of disturbing Adam or bringing Guy's wrath down upon me until it was absolutely necessary. "You should be happy to see that someone's been up here."

"Why?" Nicole asked.

"Because," I said impatiently, "*ghosts don't leave footprints.* Come on. Let's take a look for ourselves before we go running to the menfolk." I brushed past her, reached for the handle of the nearest door, and flung it open.

Daylight filtered softly through the faded drapes of a long-disused bedroom. Dust sheets covered the furniture, but the rugs were rumpled and the dust on the floor was disturbed. The same held true for the next room and the next.

"Do you suppose someone else knows about the treasure?" Nicole asked.

"If your uncle didn't know about it, how could anyone else?" I looked up and down the corridor suspiciously. The Wyrdhurst ghost was becoming more corporeal by the minute. "Were there a lot of little things up here, Nicole? Candlesticks, snuff boxes—things small enough to carry?"

"Yes, indeed," Nicole replied. "Uncle Dickie brought some bits downstairs when he refurbished our rooms, but left the rest for us to sort through. Why?"

"Let me think for a minute." My mind flashed back to the strange behavior I'd encountered at Her Majesty's pub, the averted eyes, young James's embarrassment, Bart Little's overwarm welcome. At the time I'd suspected the men of impersonating the Wyrdhurst ghost, but now another explanation seemed possible.

"If you ask me," I said, "we're dealing with a simple, straightforward case of burglary."

Nicole bristled. "Do you mean to say that someone's been looting my house under my very nose?"

I nodded. "It wouldn't be the first time thieves robbed a mansion while it was occupied."

"But how could anyone get in? We have a security system that . . ." She wilted slightly. "That I sometimes forget to use."

I pursed my lips. The Little family was looking guiltier by the minute. Who would know the Hollanders' habits better than the villagers? Guy had already proved that the locals knew all about Jared's comings and goings, and I had little doubt that Nicole's negligence was also common knowledge. News traveled fast in places like Blackhope.

Nicole stepped past me, murmuring, "Jared will be livid when he finds out what I've done."

"Maybe he shouldn't go away quite so often," I muttered, but Nicole didn't seem to hear me. She'd moved on to the last room in the east wing and was standing in the doorway, one hand raised to her mouth.

"Lori," she said. "We've found the nursery."

CHAPTER

Dusk had fallen, but a last vestige of sunlight cast striped shadows from the nursery's barred windows onto the serviceable linoleum floor.

The room was simply furnished and the walls were wainscoted in oak. Above the oak panels a painted parade of gallant steeds pranced around the room. A circle of fair damsels decorated the hearth rug.

Apart from the horses and the damsels, the room was strangely devoid of personality. The cupboards were empty, the tables bare, as if the room had been stripped of anything that might suggest the presence of children—or anything that might fetch a good price on the open market.

"Where are the dustcovers?" Nicole asked.

"Tossed in the corner," I said, pointing. "The thieves must

have left in a hurry. They didn't have time to tidy up after themselves."

"I believe the night nursery is through here," Nicole said, opening a connecting door.

The night nursery was equally anonymous. The nanny's corner held a full-sized bed, a dressing table, a washstand, and a sizable clothes cupboard. A child's bed sat opposite the nanny's, its carved headboard touching the wall. The night nursery's dust sheets lay in a heap between the child's bed and the windows.

My heart ached when I caught sight of the small bed. I could almost see Claire curled beneath a quilted counterpane, watching moonlight silver passing clouds and dreaming of the knight in shining armor who would one day carry her away.

I wandered to the windows, to look out over the darkening moors. The rising moon was nearly full, but clouds were moving in swiftly from the east. With a sigh, I turned to examine the carved headboard, caught my toe in a tangled dustcover, threw my hands out to save myself, and fell headlong through the paneled wall.

"Lori? *Lori!*" Nicole exclaimed. "Where are you?"

"I . . . I'm not sure." I pushed myself up on my hands and knees, then got to my feet. A sheet of wood the size of a small door lay beneath me, snapped cleanly from its adjoining panels. "I dropped my light."

Nicole ducked through the opening, held her flashlight high, and gasped.

I gasped with her.

"Aladdin's cave," she breathed.

"No," I said. "Claire's."

The windowless storeroom had the wan, neglected air of an abandoned toy shop. It was filled with cupboards and shelves, and every inch of space appeared to be crammed with children's things.

There were music boxes, marionettes, puzzles, and hoops; tea sets, clockwork toys, and china figurines. There were prams and cradles and dolls of all descriptions, from the humblest yarn-haired rag doll to the haughtiest porcelain-faced queen. A proscenium-arched puppet theater sat on the stone floor between a spotted rocking horse and a dollhouse furnished from scullery to attics with exquisite miniatures.

My flashlight lay between the wheels of an elegant wicker pram. I bent to retrieve it, leaving Nicole to clear a trail to the nearest cupboard.

"Lori," she said. "Look!"

She'd found a wardrobe fit for a princess: fur-trimmed dresses, lace dresses, and beaded velvet ones; hats billowing with ostrich feathers; ermine cloaks, frilled petticoats, and boxes spilling over with kid gloves, embroidered handker-chiefs, and silk stockings.

"Valenciennes lace," Nicole crooned, lifting a petticoat from a shelf.

I shone my flashlight slowly over the gorgeous fabrics, marveling at the love Josiah had showered on his only daugh-ter, the child of his old age. It was difficult to believe that a man who'd bestowed such riches upon a child had also held her captive in a barren cell.

Cold fingers seemed to brush my neck. I trembled, turned, and swept the storeroom with my flashlight. Its beam came to rest, almost of its own accord, on a large, dustcover-draped painting half hidden by a cupboard on the far side of the chamber. While Nicole inspected the petticoat's fine needlework, I allowed myself to be drawn, as if by an unseen hand, across the room.

I pulled the painting from behind the cupboard, leaned it against the dollhouse, twitched the dust sheet from its gilded frame, and saw a face I'd seen before.

She was dressed all in white, her slight frame overwhelmed by a frilled and beribboned morning gown. She had luminous dark eyes, and her raven hair, bound in a knot on the top of her head, was so thick and luxurious that it seemed too heavy for her slender neck to bear. She sat demurely, her left hand crossed gracefully over her right, a fringed shawl draped around her narrow shoulders.

"Nicole," I whispered. The resemblance was uncanny.

"Yes?" Nicole turned toward me, gasped, and clutched the petticoat to her breast. "That's—that's the face I saw! The face at the window!"

"You must have seen your own reflection." I looked from the young woman in the portrait to the young woman standing before me. "You look so much alike, you could be sisters."

Nicole crossed the room hesitantly. "Is it . . . Claire?"

I squatted to read the engraved plate mounted on the gilded frame. "Claire Eleanora Byrd. This is your great-aunt, Nicole. This is the woman Edward loved."

"Josiah must have loved her, too." Nicole looked down at the petticoat. "He must have built this room after she died, to hold every precious thing her hands had touched."

He loved her too much, I thought, gazing into Claire's dark eyes. That's why he locked her away. He couldn't bear to lose his princess to anyone, much less to a man without title or fortune.

"Adam will want to see this." I nodded silently to Claire, lifted the portrait from the floor, and carried it out of the concealed storeroom.

"He must be deeply asleep," Nicole said. "Perhaps we shouldn't disturb him."

We stood outside the blue room, with the portrait propped between us, waiting for Adam to respond to my insistent knocking. I ignored Nicole's polite suggestion, and knocked once more before putting my head inside the room.

"Adam," I called. "Wake up. We've found something really special."

I waited a scant half-second for a reply, and when none came, pushed the door wide open. Adam was nowhere in sight, and the bed looked as if it hadn't been slept in.

"He must have changed his mind about the nap," Nicole remarked.

I thought it more likely that he'd been robbed of sleep by the same tortured thoughts that had driven him to my room in the wee hours. I glanced worriedly at the smooth bedclothes, hefted the portrait, and headed for the main staircase.

I knew where we'd find Adam. He'd be in the library, brooding over Edward's letters.

The library was dark and empty, and the letters lay where we'd left them, on the low table between the sofa and the armchair.

I dropped my flashlight on the sofa, propped the portrait against a chair, and crossed to the oak table, to light a reading lamp, but before my hand touched the switch, I sensed movement beyond the darkened windows.

I stared hard, gooseflesh prickling all up and down my arms, and glimpsed an indistinct shape sliding past the terrace balustrade.

"Nicole," I said in a low voice. "Call Guy. Tell him we have an intruder. Then find the Hatches and stay with them." She started to protest, but I silenced her with a glance.

As soon as she'd gone, I walked stealthily to the terrace door and peered through the wavy panes of glass. Scudding clouds obscured the moon, but a fleeting beam showed a darker patch against the mausoleum's looming shadow. Someone was out there.

I couldn't wait for Guy, nor did I need to. My eyes were accustomed to the dark, I was dressed all in black, and I was familiar with the garden's layout. What's more, my dander was up. I didn't intend to confront anyone, but I was determined to get close enough to identify the creep who'd been giving Nicole nightmares. When clouds buried the moon, I opened the door, crept silently across the terrace, and made my way across the tangled garden.

I scuttled in a half-crouch along the weed-grown path, intent on catching sight of Nicole's tormentor before he fled into the night. When I reached the mausoleum, I paused to reconnoiter. My flesh crept as I touched the fluttering ivy, and my heart nearly stopped when a hand closed round my mouth and yanked me backward.

"What the *hell* are you doing here?" Guy's furious whisper was nearly drowned out by the roar of my thundering heart. "Shhh . . . Listen."

I couldn't do much else with Guy's left arm wrapped like

an iron band around my waist and his right hand still clamped over my mouth, so I strained my ears to hear whatever sound had caught his attention.

A moment later, I heard it: a faint moan that seemed to come from *inside* the mausoleum.

If my constitution had been one-tenth as delicate as Jared had once claimed, I would've keeled over in a dead faint then and there. Fortunately, I was the mother of twins.

"Mrrph?" I said softly.

"Quiet," Guy commanded, sotto voce. "Stay behind me."

He loosed his holds and took off, stopping when he reached the mausoleum's entrance. A great swag of ivy had been pulled aside, like a curtain, to reveal a pedimented entryway flanked by fluted columns.

The door between the columns hung open, but the darkness within was impenetrable. A second moan, louder than the first, emerged from the inky blackness, and this time I recognized the voice.

"Adam!" I cried. "Guy, give me a light. Quickly—he's hurt!"

Guy passed a penlight to me, then grabbed my arms. "I must go," he said. "Get Chase into the house and *stay there*. Your lives may depend on it."

I switched the penlight on in time to see Guy sprint along the path Adam and I had taken the day before. Guy's fair hair was covered by a black beret, his face daubed with weird streaks of grease paint, and he wore camouflage fatigues. He seemed to be dressed for combat, but I had no time to wonder why.

Adam needed me.

He lay in a heap near a crypt in the darkest corner of the

mausoleum, groaning and clutching his ribs. Blood dripped from his nose, his lips were split and bleeding, and his left eye was badly bruised.

I dropped to my knees beside him, reached out to caress his hair, touched dampness, and brought my fingers back, bloodstained. I gasped softly and wiped my hand on my sleeve.

"It's okay, Adam," I said, bending low. "I'm here."

"Lori?" His voice was slurred but urgent, and he spat blood as he spoke. "Get away from here. They'll . . . they'll . . ."

"No, they won't," I said, to quiet him. "Guy's gone after them. Come on, now. Let's get you out of this horrible place."

I slung his arm around my shoulders and helped him to his feet, but it was slow going after that. We were scarcely two steps beyond the porticoed door when the sky exploded.

A deafening roar knocked us to the ground and the horizon lit up like Armageddon. Blinding flashes peppered the sky, like fireworks run amok, and the clouds were cobwebbed with shimmering streamers that screamed as they fractured the air. Great gouts of flame geysered skyward and shock waves rippled over us as rolling thunder swept in off the moors to crash against Wyrdhurst's stone walls. Behind us, the library's windows imploded in a thousand shattered shards.

I crawled to Adam, who'd half risen to his knees to gaze at the blazing sky.

"A beautiful nightmare," he murmured.

The phrase was Edward's and I knew now what he'd meant by it. The light show was spectacular, the fear it engendered strangely exhilarating. The moment would have

been magical if not for the distant crack of rifle fire, the stac-
cato bursts of automatic weapons.

"Get . . . to house." Adam winced as he sagged to the
ground. "Safer . . . there."

The mausoleum looked pretty good to me, but Adam
needed medical attention, and I knew that Guy was handling
whatever hell had broken loose upon the moors. The explosions were already fading to a distant, scattered popping
when I took Adam's weight on my shoulders and half carried
him back into Wyrdhurst.

CHAPTER

I sat up with Adam long after Dr. MacEwan had come and gone. It was nearly dawn when Nicole crept in, as quietly as a ghost, and sent me off to bed.

Adam had bruised ribs, a mild concussion, a black eye, twenty stitches in his head, and a lot more than twenty bruises on the rest of his body. Dr. MacEwan summed up his condition by saying, "He'll survive, though there'll be moments when he'll wish he hadn't."

Adam had barely spoken after we'd come in from the garden, so I still had no idea who'd beaten him up and dumped him in the mausoleum. But I had my suspicions. Adam was the kind of man who'd risk his neck to save a flannel bunny. It wasn't hard to envision him taking on a gang of burglars singlehanded. My guess was that he'd seen them breaking into old Josiah's tomb and tried to stop them. He'd been foolishly, splendidly heroic, and he'd paid the price.

I had my suspicions about the massive explosions as well—an artillery exercise gone awry, the accidental detonation of an ammunition dump—but since I hadn't seen or heard from Guy after he'd run off into the night, I knew nothing for certain.

Mrs. Hatch was with Adam when I looked in just after noon. Major Ted was with him, too, standing to attention on the bedside table, as if protecting a wounded comrade. Adam was still deeply asleep, his head swathed in stark white bandages, his left eye swollen shut, his pale, heart-shaped face cruelly battered. I wanted to hold his hand, to let him know I was there, but I didn't want to wake him, so I slipped out of the room and made my way downstairs.

I came upon Nicole in the dining room, surveying the linen-draped table with a critical eye. A silver bowl dripping with ferns and red roses served as the centerpiece, and three places had been set with gold-rimmed china.

My hostess had devoted as much thought to dressing herself as she had to dressing the table. She looked charming in a white taffeta blouse and a swirly red tartan skirt trimmed at the hem with black velvet.

"Are we expecting company?" I asked.

"Captain Manning called while you were asleep. He wished to speak with us, so I invited him to lunch. He should be here at any moment." Nicole made her way around the table, tweaking a fork here, nudging a knife there. "We're having roast beef and Yorkshire pudding. It was Edward's favorite, you remember, and I thought that, as a soldier, Captain Manning might . . ." She looked at me anxiously, more concerned about pleasing her guest than curious about the nature of his visit.

"He'll love it," I assured her.

Our colloquy was interrupted by Hatch, announcing the captain's arrival.

"Punctual, as always," Nicole murmured. She faced the doorway, smiling in anticipation, but the moment she caught sight of the captain, her smile faded.

"Guy," she said, her voice trembling. "You're hurt."

Guy was nearly as pale as Adam. His gray eyes were smudged with fatigue, lines of strain creased his brow, and his left arm was bound up in a sling.

"It's nothing, Mrs. Hollander," he demurred, but Mrs. Hollander disagreed.

"Don't be absurd," she snapped. "If it were nothing, your poor arm wouldn't be in a great enormous sling."

I stood back while Nicole swung into action, guiding Guy to the head of the table and ordering Hatch to bring a cushion from the sitting room. She offered brandy, but Guy declined.

"If I'd known you were hurt, I wouldn't have asked you to come here," she said, gently settling his arm on the cushion.

"I wanted to come," he told her. "I have information that concerns you. I wanted to be the one to—"

"You're not to say another word until you've had a bite to eat." Nicole gestured for me to take my seat and signaled for Hatch to serve the meal. "You look as weak as a kitten. When was the last time you had a proper meal?"

"I assure you, Mrs. Holl—"

"Not a word," Nicole scolded.

I smiled reminiscently as Nicole fussed over him, re-membering my first meal with Adam, when he'd taken the soup spoon from my shaking hand and fed me like a baby. It seemed a hundred years ago, though it had been only six days.

Guy endured Nicole's hovering with admirable forti-tude, and the roast beef did him a world of good, but when Nicole insisted that he rest in one of the guest rooms after lunch, he took a stand. Nicole gave in gracefully, telling Hatch that we'd take coffee in the library.

The explosions on the moors had shattered three of the room's tall windows, but Hatch had already boarded them up and Mrs. Hatch had cleared away the glass. As Hatch served the coffee, I saw that someone had moved my flashlight and Edward's letters to the oak table, and leaned Claire's portrait against the massive, clouded mirror atop the mantelpiece.

Claire's portrait faced Josiah's across the long room, and for a moment, the face-off discomfited me. It was as if Josiah were still spying on his daughter, still pinning her with his cold, intrusive gaze.

The longer I looked at Claire, though, the more certain I became that her portrait was exactly where it should be. I could see her expression more clearly here than in the sealed storeroom. Her gaze was less demure, far more defiant than I remembered it, as if she were letting her father know that she'd finally escaped the prison of his possessive love.

"Lori," Nicole remonstrated, "will you please stop star-ing at my great-aunt and attend to what Captain Manning has to say? I'm sure it's of the utmost importance."

I came out of my trance and sat beside Nicole on the sofa. Hatch was gone and Guy was in the armchair nearest the hearth, his wounded arm resting on a tasseled pillow in his lap, his booted feet propped on a leather ottoman.

"It's a rather complicated story," Guy warned, "one you may find difficult to believe."

"I'll believe whatever you tell me, Captain Manning," said Nicole.

Guy acknowledged her pledge by addressing his opening remarks to her. He spoke calmly and directly, a professional soldier delivering hard facts.

"A year ago, when the refurbishment of Wyrdhurst Hall commenced, someone started a campaign designed to make you and your husband feel unwelcome in the village of Blackhope and uncomfortable in your new home. . . ."

Guy quickly recapitulated the information he'd passed on to me beside the church in Blackhope. He described the flowers left before Clive Aynsworth's memorial, the building of the Guy Fawkes Day bonfire within sight of Wyrdhurst's towers, the revived rumors of the schoolteacher's murder, and the resurrection of the Wyrdhurst ghost.

"Someone even went so far as to re-create the ghost," he told Nicole. "The noises you heard at night, Mrs. Hollander, were quite real."

"I know." Nicole's head bobbed eagerly. "Lori thinks they were made by burglars."

"I'm afraid we're dealing with something far more serious than burglary," said Guy. "Those noises were, like the rumors, part of a plot to force you to abandon your home."

Nicole looked perplexed. "Why would anyone want me to leave Wyrdhurst?"

"You were in the way." Guy took a careful breath and

eased his arm into a more comfortable position on the pillow before dropping a bomb every bit as unexpected as the explosions that had shattered the windows. "For the past three years, Mrs. Hollander, Wyrdhurst has been used as a weapons cache by a band of terrorists bent on assaulting and destroying the Scottish Parliament."

Nicole's mouth fell open and a long moment passed.

"Terrorists?" I croaked.

"I rather think I preferred ghosts," Nicole said weakly.

"Forgive me," said Guy. "I know how upsetting this must be for you."

Nicole lifted her chin. "It's far less upsetting than not knowing the truth. Do go on."

Guy bowed to her wishes. "Three years ago Wyrdhurst was, to all intents and purposes, an abandoned ruin. Its isolation and its proximity to the Scottish border made it an ideal place to store the weapons and high explosives the group was slowly acquiring."

"Do you mean to tell me," Nicole broke in, "that my husband and I have been living in a house filled with high explosives?"

"I'm afraid so," Guy said.

Nicole gave a hiccuping giggle, cleared her throat, and told Guy to continue.

"Wyrdhurst's proximity to the artillery range was also an advantage." He turned to me. "The strange rock formation you and Chase discovered on the moors is, in fact, a full-scale mockup of the floor plan of the Scottish Parliament building in Edinburgh. Those involved in the plot used it to practice and time their takeover maneuvers."

"Good grief," I muttered, but the more I thought about it, the more sense it made. The army didn't fire on the quadrant nearest Wyrdhurst, and the range as a whole was barred to civilians. As long as they stayed near Wyrdhurst, the terrorists wouldn't have to worry about being bombarded by the army or interrupted by casual hikers.

Guy paused for a sip of coffee before continuing. "The hall's refurbishment took them by surprise," he said. "None of the locals knew what was happening until the first work crews arrived on site."

Nicole flushed. "It was a rather sudden decision on my uncle's part," she confessed. "I asked him to give me Wyrdhurst as a wedding present."

The flicker of pain in Guy's eyes had nothing to do with his arm, but he masked it with another sip of coffee.

I gave him a moment before asking, "Why didn't Dickie's workmen find the weapons?"

"Most of the weapons were cached in the dungeons," he explained.

"Which have yet to be cleared of rubbish," Nicole said, sighing.

"Correct." Guy drained his cup and returned it to the table at his elbow. "Once the refurbishment began, the presence of so many work crews, working round the clock, made it impossible for the miscreants to retrieve their materiel. Afterwards, Mr. Hollander's excellent security system foiled their attempts."

Nicole studiously avoided Guy's gaze as she refilled his cup, but she couldn't avoid what was coming next.

Guy pulled no punches. "It took the men very little time

to discover that, during your husband's absences, Mrs. Hollander, you failed to utilize the security system properly. You made it easy for them to come in through the terrace door. Once inside, they made their way to the dungeons via a circuitous but secure route, which they'd discovered before the hall was occupied."

"The secret staircase?" I hazarded.

Guy confirmed my guess. The intruders had used the staircase to reach Jared's conveniently unoccupied bedroom. From there, they'd gone down the servants' stairs to the dungeons.

"They went to the third floor as well," Nicole reminded Guy. "They tromped around up there repeatedly, for the sole purpose of frightening me."

Guy tugged on an earlobe. "They deny doing so more than once," he said. "But it's early days yet. I expect further interrogation to elicit further details. By the way," he added, "the laughter you heard, Lori, was made by a recording device installed by one of the group."

I found it interesting that Guy had so far avoided referring to the terrorists by name. Was it because the names would mean nothing to us, I wondered, or because one name would mean too much? If Jared was involved in or even aware of the plot, Guy would find himself in an extremely awkward position. How did one tell the woman one loved that her husband was a criminal?

"Guy," I said, with a sidelong glance at Nicole, "you mentioned interrogations. Have you caught the thugs?"

"We caught them last night," he said. "Your accident, in fact, led directly to their capture."

"The gate." I made a wry face as the penny dropped. "They opened the gate to the military track, and forgot to close it."

"A small but significant mistake," Guy observed. "It was the gate that drew my attention to the plot."

Guy had known from the start that none of his men would have left the gate open, and he'd set out to prove it. He'd lifted the imprint of a tire from the muddy track, and used it to identify a nonmilitary vehicle. It had taken him two days to identify the vehicle's current owner.

"Tell us his name," Nicole demanded.

I held my breath.

"Bart Little," Guy replied.

"The publican?" I exclaimed.

"Mr. Little asked me to apologize to you, Lori." The merest hint of irony crept into Guy's voice. "He thinks it unsporting to harm women."

"What about the women in Parliament?" Nicole asked.

"Consistency is not a trait one usually associates with fanatics." Guy gingerly crossed his legs. "I didn't know it at the time, but the landlord of Her Majesty's pub is also a rabid ultranationalist. He and a small band of followers believe that Britain's greatness has been vitiated by the devolution of power to Scotland, Wales, and Northern Ireland. Mr. Little considers himself a patriot. Hence his respect for the military."

In my mind's eye, I saw the Union Jack hanging above Her Majesty's bar, along with the color portraits of the queen and the heirs apparent. Recalling our red-carpet treatment, I murmured, "Lunch is on the house, Captain Manning."

Guy allowed himself a brief, humorless smile. "It was the

perfect cover," he conceded. "A publican is very like an intelligence officer, keeping abreast of local happenings that might affect his operations."

Guy told us that Bart Little had placed the call to Adam's publisher, hoping to glean information about the mysterious stranger who'd rented the fishing hut. While Mr. Little gathered information on the ground, his son James scoured the Net for weapons suppliers. James had also rigged the tape recorder that had given me such a scare.

"The boy is adept at electronics," Guy noted. "He regarded the device as something of a joke."

No one in the room was laughing. Nicole looked stunned, the captain disgusted. I felt a strange mixture of relief and self-reproach. In light of what Guy had just told us, my suspicions about Jared seemed childish. I was glad I'd never shared them with Nicole, and ashamed of myself for suspecting him in the first place. Nicole's husband might be a pompous prig, but he wasn't evil.

"Before I could question Mr. Little about the gate," Guy said, "my men spotted him coming up the military track in a small van—the same van whose imprint I'd taken. I ordered them to keep out of sight."

Guy wanted to find out what was going on. He followed Bart and three of his men from the military track all the way to Wyrdhurst's dungeons, where he watched them retrieve three wooden crates. When they'd gone, he opened the few that remained.

"They contained automatic weapons," Guy informed us. "We learned subsequently that the explosives had already been removed."

"Thank heavens," Nicole said fervently.

"I'd just alerted my men," Guy continued, "when your call came through, Mrs. Hollander, telling me that Lori had spotted an intruder."

"Adam must have spotted them first," I said. "That's why he went to the mauso—"

"Did they hide *weapons* in the *mausoleum*?" Nicole interrupted, her voice quivering with outrage.

"They won't admit to it," Guy acknowledged, "but as I said, it's early days."

I turned to Nicole. "I'll bet Adam came downstairs to reread Edward's letters, saw men who appeared to be carrying boxes away from the mausoleum, and tried to stop them."

"It was a damned silly thing to do," Guy said brusquely. "He could have been killed. You both could have been killed, and it would have been left to me to notify your next of kin."

"I'm sorry," I said, head bowed and heart clenching.

"Can't we allow Adam and Lori a little bravery?" Nicole coaxed. "I think they were trying to protect me."

"We were all—" Guy's voice broke. He took a long draft of coffee before adding gruffly, "We were all concerned for your well-being, Mrs. Hollander."

Nicole's large eyes grew solemn. "What happened on the moors last night, Captain Manning?"

"War." Guy's mouth tightened, and the lines around his eyes deepened. "I don't know what else to call it. My men were lying in wait, ready to take Mr. Little into custody for the illegal possession of firearms. We intended to do so peacefully, but he and his men fired upon us, and somehow set off the explosive devices in the van. The van's driver was killed—a Mr. Garnett."

"The mechanic." I put a hand to my mouth, aghast. "He tried to keep Adam away from Wyrdhurst by telling him about the ghost."

"He also put the flowers in front of Mr. Aynsworth's memorial and proposed moving the bonfire to its old site," Guy said. "He was the only other villager involved in the plot, though I dare say a few knew that something untoward was going on."

"And your men?" Nicole asked gently. "Was anyone else wounded, besides you?"

"Fortunately not," said Guy. "But the moors have soaked up another dead man's blood. I truly regret it."

Guy fell silent, gazing past us through the windows, as if he could still see fire in the sky. For a moment I forgot his rank and was aware only of a very young man burdened with awful responsibilities, a man not much older than Edward had been when he'd gone to war.

"Is it the first time you've been wounded?" I asked.

Guy's smile was heart-wrenching. "I've never been shot at before. I've never been in combat. I never imagined that my enemy would also be my countryman." He ran his tongue along his lips, as though his mouth had suddenly gone dry. "As he took aim at me, he called me a traitor."

"How *dare*—" Nicole's heated protest ended abruptly when the study doors flew open and Dickie Byrd burst into the room.

"What the devil is going on?" Dickie was red-faced and bristling, a bantam rooster itching for a fight. "Nickie, love, are you okay?"

"Uncle Dickie?" she said, blinking in disbelief. "What are you doing here?"

"I heard that all hell had broken loose up here." Dickie caught sight of the boarded windows and rounded on Guy. "If you're to blame for this shambles, my lad, I'll have something to say to your commanding officer."

Nicole jumped to her feet and boldly interposed herself between Guy and her pugnacious uncle. "How *dare* you, Uncle Dickie! I'll have you know that Captain Guy Manning is the kindest, bravest, most courageous, best, and most admirable man who ever lived. What's more, he's *punctual!*"

Dickie Byrd listened thoughtfully to his niece's furious tirade, then looked past her at Guy. "You married, young man?"

"No, sir," Guy replied with amazing self-possession. "But your niece is."

"That's about to change." Dickie gripped Nicole's shoulders and looked her square in the face. "Wait till you hear what your worthless lump of a husband has been up to in Newcastle." He turned toward the study doors and bellowed, "Jared! Get your bum in here!"

CHAPTER

Jared Hollander slunk into the room like a dog caught digging up a flower bed. He was dressed as beautifully as ever, but his bluff manner and arrogant posturing had vanished. He walked head-down, refusing to make eye contact with anyone in the room except for Dickie, whom he eyed nervously.

Dickie placed a straight-backed wooden chair before the hearth, pointed to it, and barked, "Sit."

Jared sat.

Dickie then took the floor, strutting between the hearth and the oak table like a prosecuting attorney presenting a summation.

"I've never liked you, Jared," he began. "I liked you even less after you began your little trips to Newcastle. What kind of man leaves his wife alone in the back end of nowhere, less than three months into his marriage? That's what I asked myself, and that's why I hired a private detective—to get some answers."

Jared sank lower in his chair.

"You thought you could treat Nicole like a child," Dickie continued. "You could teach her, scold her, mold her, but you couldn't really love her, could you, Jared?" He placed his face three inches from Jared's and repeated sharply, *"Could you?"*

"No," Jared whispered.

Nicole's eyelashes fluttered in confusion and Dickie came to stand before her.

"I'm sorry, love," he said, "but I swore on your father's grave that I'd look after you, and that's what I'm doing." He glared at Jared. "Do you want to tell her what my detective discovered, or shall I?"

"Please," said Jared. "Allow me. I owe her that much."

"You owe her a damned sight—" Dickie began, but Nicole silenced him with a touch.

"Let Jared speak," she said. She looked imploringly at her husband. "Is it true, Jared? Is it true that you never loved me?"

"There are all kinds of love," Jared answered. "You and I share a love of beautiful things, Nicole, and I greatly admire your gentleness. It's rare to find a woman so lovely and yet so untouched by the world. In you, I knew I'd found a pearl of great price."

For the first time, I caught a glimpse of what Nicole saw in her husband. Jared's declaration held a softness and sincerity I'd never imagined him to possess. Guy, for his part, had eyes for no one but Nicole. He slid the pillow from his lap and watched her almost without blinking, as if poised to come to her defense.

Jared stared down at his hands. "I hoped that one day I

might come to love you as you deserve to be loved, but it was no good. It was never any good." He took a deep breath. "The truth is, Nicole, I'm in love with someone else."

Nicole's lower lip trembled. "I see."

"No, Nickie, you don't see," Dickie insisted. "Ask him who he's in love with."

"Jared?" Nicole prompted.

Jared twisted his hands in his lap. "His name is Karl. He teaches art therapy at Newcastle General. I met him shortly after you and I became engaged. I didn't mean to fall in love with him, but . . ." One shoulder rose in a minute gesture of resignation.

"Karl . . ." Nicole tilted her head to one side and gazed abstractedly into the middle distance. "His name is Karl. *His* name is Karl. I see. I truly do see now. That's why we never . . . Oh, yes, I do see your predicament." She favored him with a pitying smile. "Poor Jared."

"Poor *Jared*?" Dickie thundered.

Jared stiffened and some of his pomposity returned. "Thank you for understanding, Nicole. Your uncle, alas, is somewhat homophobic."

"I don't care if you snog *parrots!*" Dick retorted. "But you don't get to lie about it, my lad. You don't get to pretend you're someone you're not. And you sure as hell don't get to marry my niece!"

Jared withered under the onslaught. "You're quite right, Mr. Byrd. My behavior toward Nicole has been reprehensible. If there was any way I could make it up to her, I would."

Nicole got to her feet. There was something regal in her bearing as she walked slowly to her husband, placed her hand under his chin, and lifted it until she could look into his eyes.

"You will leave Wyrdhurst," she said evenly. "I'll see to it that your things are sent on, and Uncle Dickie will take care of the annulment." She let her hand drop and took a backward step, as if making way for his departure. "Please give Karl my best. I hope the two of you will be very happy."

Jared rose, tweaked the waxed tips of his mustache, and left the room. Hatch, no doubt under Dickie's orders, met him at the study doors to escort him from the premises.

The moment Hatch closed the doors Nicole covered her face with her hands and began to sob. Guy leapt to his feet and gathered her to him, encircling her with his good arm while she buried her face in his sling.

Dickie started toward them, but I grabbed his elbow and hauled him toward the hidden stairs.

"Don't you know when to make an exit?" I scolded, reaching for my flashlight. "Come with me. I've got books to show you."

It's not every day that a mother, wife, and part-time bibliographer gets to captivate a corporate titan, but not many mothers, wives, or bibliographers are blessed with such riveting material.

By the time I finished telling my tale of terrorists, ghosts, and tragic wartime romance, Dickie was as close to speechless as I'd ever seen him. Which wasn't really very close.

"Captain Manning took a bullet defending my girl, did he?" Dickie crossed the tower room to peer out of a narrow window. "I like the sound of that."

"He's a genuinely good man," I said. "Nicole could do a lot worse."

"She already has," Dickie asserted. He turned his back to the window and let his gaze travel slowly around the room. "Truth to tell, I can understand Josiah's feelings. When Nickie decided to leave me for that lying lump, I wanted to lock her up. But I knew I couldn't. You've got to let them fly, don't you? That's why I didn't look into Jared sooner. I didn't want to set a foot wrong, have her accuse me of interfering." He sighed. "But I think I know how the old devil felt."

When I broached the subject of ghosts, Dickie claimed that he'd encountered a variety of apparitions in musty libraries and dusty bookshops all over England. He didn't bat an eye when I told him that Wyrdhurst was haunted. I didn't tell him everything Claire had done, only that she'd needed my help to solve her problems.

"You're not done yet," he commented. "You still have to find the treasure Edward sent." He glanced at his watch, then gave me a grim look of disapproval. "We've been up here for two hours and I haven't seen a single book. If you've lied to me, I'll have something to say to Stan Finderman."

We spent another hour exploring in the cupboard. Dickie was so delighted with the children's books that he promised to add an endowment to the Serenissima as payment for my services. Stan Finderman would, I knew, have something flattering to say about his protégé's success.

Nicole was sitting at Guy's knee when Dickie and I came through the hidden door. The two were so absorbed in each other that they didn't notice us until Dickie let loose a stentorian *"Ahem!"*

"Uncle Dickie?" Nicole's eyes were reddened from crying, but she seemed well on the way to a full recovery. "Where have you been?"

"Looking at books." Dickie extended his hand to Guy. "Lori's told me everything you've done for my niece—and for my country. It's a privilege to know you, sir."

"The privilege is mine," Guy returned.

"I've thanked Guy for sending Adam to watch over us," Nicole told me brightly.

Guy's eyes slid toward me. "It was such a remarkably fine idea that I'm surprised I managed to think of it."

"I'm not," Nicole said. "You're brilliant as well as brave."

"I'm also very late." Guy stood. "I'm afraid I must be going."

"I'll drive you," offered Dickie. "Make sure you get there in one piece. My man can ferry your car."

Nicole decided to accompany the men, but I declined her invitation to join them. I needed some time to myself.

I sat alone before Claire's portrait, sifting through myriad small details that until now had seemed utterly unconnected. Slowly, carefully, I arranged and rearranged the pieces of the puzzle until a picture began to emerge. Finally, I put in a call to Dr. MacEwan. It took him less than five minutes to answer my questions.

By then Dickie and Nicole had returned, in a festive mood. For the moment, I set the puzzle aside and joined them in their celebration. There'd been more than enough revelations for one day. I would wait until tomorrow to fit the final pieces into place.

CHAPTER

24

I put off seeing Adam until after lunch the next day, when Nicole took Dickie upstairs to examine young Claire's things, and the risk of interruption was remote.

The drapes were open in the blue room, and the windows framed a dark, forbidding sky. Adam was sitting up in bed, the covers smoothed to his waist, his back propped against a mound of pillows. His attire was uncharacteristically flamboyant—a pair of watered silk pajamas in a squint-worthy shade of bottle-green.

He looked very frail. His blackened left eye was swollen shut and his face bore the marks of his beating, but when he turned his head to smile at me, my heart still took off at a gallop.

"I hope you don't intend to amuse me," he said. "It hurts like hell when I laugh."

"I guess that rules out my opening remarks on your jammies," I said.

"They're Jared's," he informed me dryly. "Nicole insisted. She was in here earlier, telling me the most hair-raising tale about Guy Manning saving the world from bloodthirsty fanatics. It seems to have had a happy ending, though. She's clearly besotted."

"The feeling's mutual. He's over the moon." I crossed to the right side of the bed, to sit in the chair Mrs. Hatch had provided for visitors, but before I could take a seat, Adam patted the blankets.

"Come up here," he said. "I'm getting a sore neck from turning my head in one direction."

I kicked off my shoes, climbed gingerly onto the massive bed, and sat facing him, my back against the footboard, wondering where to begin.

"We always seem to end up in bed together," I said with a rueful grin.

"Yes." Adam sighed wistfully. "It's a pity we're such an honorable pair."

I laughed and looked toward the windows. "I got it all wrong, you know. First I thought it was Jared, trying to scare Nicole. Then I thought it might be the charwomen he'd insulted, or villagers acting on their behalf. I even came up with a theory about burglars." I shook my head. "I never suspected terrorists."

"It would have been very strange if you had," Adam commented. "It's Guy's job to think of such things, not yours."

"Right. It's just . . ." I caught my lower lip between my teeth. "I'm not sure his job's done. There are some loose ends that have been bugging the heck out of me."

"What sort of loose ends?" Adam asked.

"I'm not happy with Bart Little's confession." I pulled my knees to my chest and wrapped my arms around them. "He admits to big things, like plotting to blow up the Scottish Parliament, but denies all sorts of little things."

"Can you be more specific?" Adam requested.

I concentrated on my clasped hands. "He says his men went to the third floor only once, but Nicole heard someone up there at least three times. He says his men never touched the dustcovers up there, but someone did. And there's something else . . ."

Adam said nothing.

"Bart denies going into the mausoleum," I continued, still staring at my hands. "He swears that he ran into you as you were coming out of the tomb."

"Does he?" Adam said softly.

The hint of resignation in his voice told me that I was on the right track. I would rather have been anyplace else, but there was no turning back. I had to know the truth, for Claire's sake, and my own.

"And . . . and there's the face Nicole saw at her bedroom window," I faltered, "and the flying ghost outside of the library. There's the block and tackle on the east tower and . . . and it took pretty good climbing skills to rescue Reginald and . . . and . . ."

"What are you trying to say, Lori?" Adam asked.

His kindly tone made me feel like a badgering brute. I ducked my head and tried to speak with more composure. "I found you lying near a crypt in the mausoleum. There's an inscription carved on the crypt. I didn't have time to take it in right then, but later it came back to me."

"It's funny what you can remember when you set your mind to it," Adam murmured.

I couldn't bring myself to meet his gaze. "Can you remember the inscription, Adam?"

"'Claire Eleanora Byrd,'" he recited. "'A tribute of affection to the memory of a beloved daughter from her afflicted father.'"

"And the dates," I pressed, though I hated myself for pressing. "I'm not usually good with numbers, but I remember the dates. Do you?"

"Born October 31, 1898," Adam said. "Released March 15, 1918. She hadn't yet turned twenty."

I forced myself to go on. "She didn't die of a broken heart, and influenza didn't kill her. I asked Dr. MacEwan to check the old medical records, but he didn't have to. He'd checked them very recently, you see. Someone else wanted to know how Claire Byrd died." I looked at Adam pleadingly, through a glaze of tears. "Who are you, Adam Chase, and why did you come to Wyrdhurst?"

Adam held my gaze for a fleeting moment, then turned his face away. "I tried to tell you—"

"I know." I recalled the melancholy glances, the half-regretful smiles, knowing that I'd gotten them wrong, too. "In the hut, after I told you about Dimity, you tried. It doesn't matter. You can tell me now."

Adam asked for water. I filled a glass from the carafe on the dressing table and brought it to him. He took a sip, cradled the glass in his hands, and began to speak.

"Once upon a time, there was a foundling. . . ."

I sank onto the chair and sat motionless. There was no

need to worry about Adam's neck. He looked straight ahead as he spoke, his eye focused on nothing.

"She was found on a moonless night on the doorstep of a cottage in Holywell. The elderly couple who took her in called her a gift from God and gave her a loving home.

"It wasn't until he lay dying that her adoptive father told her a great secret: she was the unacknowledged daughter of Claire Byrd, who'd died giving birth to her. Claire's death had driven Claire's father mad and, fearful for the child's safety, the midwife had smuggled her out of Wyrdhurst and brought her to people who would love and protect her.

"My mother . . ." The words seemed to catch in his throat and he took a moment to steady himself. "My mother didn't believe a word of it. She thought the dear man had invented a fable to comfort her, to make her feel like . . . Cinderella. That's what she told her son when she shared the tale with him many years later.

"By then her son had become something of an expert on the Great European War. He tramped the battlefields, interviewed survivors, roamed forests of white crosses. . . ." Adam sipped from the glass, set it aside, and let his head fall back against the mound of pillows. "He felt a peculiar affinity for the men who fought and died near Ypres. He combed archives for their letters, postcards, journals. He needed to hear them tell their stories in their own words."

There was a ripping sound, like a sheet being torn in two, and a torrent of rain slashed the windows, as if every cloud in the sky had opened at once. Adam turned his head to watch the downpour.

"They wrote of the rain in Ypres," he said, "the ceaseless,

murderous rain. . . ." He gave a soft sigh and faced forward. "One day the foundling's son unearthed a series of letters in an archive at the Imperial War Museum. They'd been written by a man called Peter Mitchell to his wife."

"Mitchell," I whispered, the name clicking into place. "Edward's friend."

Adam stared up at the molded plaster ceiling. "Peter Mitchell rarely wrote about the rain. He was too caught up in a friend's tale of forbidden love. One can hardly blame him for recounting every word Edward confided in him. Retelling Edward's story allowed Mitchell to escape, if only on paper, the horrors that surrounded him."

It was all there, in Peter Mitchell's letters: Edward's summers with his uncle, his work in Wyrdhurst's library, his first encounter with Claire, the sunny morning on the moors when their friendship had blossomed into love. Josiah was there, too, a menacing shadow dimming the horizon.

Mitchell couldn't understand why Josiah hadn't squelched the budding romance by sending Claire away. He concluded that Josiah was less concerned with ending the relationship than with breaking his daughter's will.

Mitchell told his wife about Clive Aynsworth's role as courier while Edward was at war, and Claire's cleverness in hiding Edward's letters. Mitchell's final letter, like Edward's, told of a treasure thrown into their laps by a stray shell.

"And there the story ended." Adam lowered his gaze to the footboard. "Peter Mitchell was killed in action ten days after he wrote to Claire. His widow eventually bequeathed his letters to the museum, where they sat, virtually untouched, until I came across them in my research."

"But you couldn't let it go at that," I said.

"No," said Adam. "I couldn't."

Adam visited Peter Mitchell's daughter, who showed him a diamond-encrusted tiara and an emerald brooch Mitchell had sent home to his wife. Adam spoke with Edward's nieces and nephews, but they had little interest in the family's past. His effects and the letters he'd sent home had long since been thrown away.

Finally, Adam contacted Dr. MacEwan, who dug up a midwife's report describing Claire Byrd's death from a condition that would today be recognized as hemorrhagic shock. The influenza rumors had been just that—rumors spread in order to avoid scandal.

"Claire died nine months after Edward's last leave." Adam's voice was calm, but strong emotions flickered just behind his eye, like distant lightning heralding a storm. "I believe she spent the greater part of those nine months locked in the west tower. I believe she died in childbirth because of the harsh conditions of her imprisonment. I also believe that, if the midwife hadn't intervened, Josiah would have killed my mother."

An image floated through my mind, of Claire huddled before the grate while cold rains whipped the tower, warming herself and the child growing within her, finding strength in Edward's words and in Josiah's sole indulgence—a cupboard full of harmless children's books.

I looked up at Adam. "Do you think Edward knew that Claire was pregnant?"

"No," Adam said softly. "I doubt that Claire knew, until after Edward was gone. By the time she realized what had happened, Josiah had killed Clive Aynsworth, and there was no one left to protect her."

The wind moaned against the windows, as if mourning for the young girl and her baby. A sense of angry, helpless grief came over me, but I pushed it aside for the moment, and steeled myself to go on.

"You came to Wyrdhurst for revenge," I said. It wasn't an accusation. I was simply trying to ascertain the facts. "The fishing hut was your base of operations. You used the block-and-tackle's rope to gain access to the hall's upper stories. It was your footsteps Nicole heard, your face at her bedroom window, you she saw 'flying' down to the terrace. You snuck into the library and read through Edward's notes while I was in Blackhope. You came here to steal the treasure."

"No." Adam's face crumpled and a tear trickled down his cheek. "I wanted Edward's letters, for my mother. I swear to you, that's all I've ever wanted."

I put a hand out to comfort him, but he waved it off.

"Don't be kind to me, Lori. I don't deserve it. I may not have intended to frighten Nicole, but I . . . I did intend to use you."

I sat back, blinking slowly. "Use me? How?"

"Do you remember that first night, when I left my shirt off?" Adam paused long enough for me to picture the fire-light warming his lean, well-sculpted torso. "I did it on purpose. I saw the way you looked at me. I wanted you to go on looking at me in that way. You were to be my key to Wyrd-hurst's many doors."

I flushed.

"I played the hero, rescuing Reginald and your luggage," he went on, his voice taut with self-disgust. "And I played the lover, flattering and caressing you—not too much and not too often, just enough to keep the kettle on the boil. I came close to kissing you on several occasions, but we were always interrupted."

I poked my head out of the pit of humiliation long enough to mutter, "We weren't interrupted on the moors."

"That's true," he agreed. "But when push came to shove, I couldn't go through with it. By then I'd come to know you—and to care for you." He gave a helpless laugh. "I intended to seduce you, Lori, but you ended up seducing me."

"Claire seduced you," I stated firmly. I allowed myself the luxury of a brief, face-saving glare before adding gruffly, "With a lot of help from me."

We sat in silence, examining our hands, taking a moment to digest the truths we'd just admitted. It didn't take me long to realize that they were the kind of truths only the closest of friends could share. I reached out to grasp Adam's hand, and he raised mine to his lips.

"Thank you," he said.

"You're welcome." I narrowed my eyes to slits. "Just don't let it happen again."

He wiped his eye with the sleeve of Jared's pajama top, then frowned slightly. "How did you know that Nicole saw me at the windows? Did she finally recognize my face?"

"No. But I did. Wait here." I stood. "I'll be right back."

I went to the corridor and returned with Claire's portrait. When I propped it at the end of Adam's bed, he seemed to melt.

"Claire," he breathed. "Where did you find her?"

"I'll show you, as soon as you're up and about." I climbed onto the bed and snuggled in beside him, sharing his mound of pillows. "I saw her resemblance to Nicole right off, but it took me a while to realize who else she reminded me of."

I looked from one face to the other and saw the same luminous dark eyes, the same fair skin, the same gleaming ebony hair—even the hands were a similar. I looked from Adam's Gypsy curls to Claire's twining tendrils and marveled that it had taken me such a long time to catch on.

"I resemble my grandfather as well." Adam slid a photograph from beneath the covers. "I found it in the regimental archives. I was looking at it when you came in."

The sepia studio portrait showed a slim young man in an overlarge uniform, standing before a painted backdrop of weeping willows. The dark-haired, dark-eyed boy looked more like a high-school student than a hardened soldier.

"You have his mouth," I said, "and his love of words. You have his build, too. That must be why Claire wanted me to . . ." I touched a fingertip to Edward's lips. "It must have been like kissing him one last time."

"It was that kind of kiss." Adam paused. "Rather an odd one to bestow on a grandson, don't you think?"

"Dimity says Claire's been insane for a long time," I reasoned. "I suppose her grandmotherly emotions got tangled up with her . . . other emotions. You do look a lot like Edward. Besides," I added, "she was filtering everything through me, and my feelings for you weren't one tiny bit grandmotherly."

"I'm glad to hear it," said Adam.

I grinned up at him, then leaned my head against his shoulder. "So what do we do now?"

"I suppose another kiss is out of the question?" Adam ventured.

"You suppose correctly. We're much too honorable." My gaze lingered on Edward's mouth. "Apart from that, it wouldn't be the same. Claire packed nearly a century of longing into that kiss."

"I'll check back with you in another hundred years, then, shall I?"

"Please do."

We spoke lightly, as if to relieve the strain of the past hour, but we both knew that we were only half kidding. We didn't need to say the words aloud to know that, in another time, another place, we would have been much more than friends.

"I'm going to tell Nicole and her uncle the truth," Adam said. "Afterwards, if they can still stand the sight of me, I'm going to offer to help them locate Edward's treasure."

I smiled at him, but there was gravity behind the smile. "If you ask me, Claire's already found her treasure."

CHAPTER

While Adam repeated his story to Nicole and Uncle Dickie, I sat in my room with the blue journal, filling Dimity in on recent events. She was disgusted by the terrorist plot, appalled by Jared's dishonesty, enchanted by Nicole's new-found love, and deeply touched by Adam's search for his grandparents.

Though an accident brought you and Adam together, it's no accident that your paths crossed here.

"What do you mean?" I asked.

Something more than books drew you to Wyrdhurst.

"As I recall, I had a bad case of cabin fever."

It wasn't just cabin fever, Lori. Think back. Didn't you feel a special something tugging you northward?

"Now that you mention it . . ." I remembered the Gypsy

in me dancing, stirred by the lure of the north's misty hills. "I guess I did."

You and Adam are uniquely qualified to heal Claire's afflicted soul. You, because your relationship to me made it possible for you to act on her behalf. Adam, because he's the answer to all of her questions.

"I'm not sure I understand," I said.

Adam may think he came to Wyrdhurst to steal Edward's letters, but I think he was brought here for quite another reason.

"What reason?" I asked.

Claire needed to know what had happened to her daughter.

A small knife twisted inside of me as I stared down at Aunt Dimity's words. Until that moment I'd hadn't grasped the full magnitude of Claire's suffering. I looked across the room to my sons' smiling faces and thought of Claire, dying in an agony of fear, terrified of what her father would do to the helpless infant she'd delivered.

"Couldn't she find her child?" I asked. "Their souls must have been linked."

As I told you before, Claire was quite mad for a very long period of time after her death. Now you know why.

I was silent for a moment, considering the desperation that had driven Claire to invade my mind. It was something only a mother could understand, and I realized that Claire had chosen me not just because of my relationship with Dimity, but because I had two children at home, for whom I would do absolutely anything.

"About these unique qualifications of mine," I said, after a time. "Is this sort of thing likely to happen again?"

No one can predict the future, Lori. That's what makes life interesting.

"My life has been a little too interesting lately," I told her. "I'm going to dig up Edward's treasure, then run straight home to my husband and kids." I looked down at the journal. "I don't suppose you know where the treasure's hidden."

The hiding place is much too obvious. You'd be embarrassed if I told you.

"Go ahead, embarrass me."

I'll give you one hint and then I must be off: Claire was an accomplished seamstress.

When the familiar loops of royal-blue ink had faded from the page, I closed the journal and leaned back on the fainting couch, to ponder Aunt Dimity's clue.

Claire's skill with the needle came as no surprise to me. There's been evidence of it everywhere in the tower room: the sewing basket, the embroidery frame, the neat stitches that had kept Edward's letters safely hidden in the mattress. I'd seen another display of fine stitchery in the dainty wardrobe Nicole had discovered in the concealed storeroom, but the storeroom wasn't what I'd call an obvious hiding place. There were too many nooks and crannies among all of the toys.

Stumped, I glanced across the room at Reginald, who sat on the bedside table, watching me sympathetically.

"Okay, Reg," I said. "If you were a treasure, where would you hide?"

The firelight danced in his black button eyes and suddenly I knew the answer. It was so excruciatingly obvious that I was, as Dimity had predicted, mortified by my failure to see it sooner. I jumped up from the couch, hoping that Nicole and Dickie were still with Adam. I wanted everyone together when I made my startling announcement.

I waited outside of Adam's door, wincing with each clap of Dickie's thunderous voice. The words "breaking and entering" were bandied about, along with "attempted robbery," "trespassing," and the truly breathtaking "reckless endangerment of a young woman's mental health." If it hurt Adam to laugh, I could only imagine how much it hurt him to endure one of Dickie's patented rants.

But Nicole was in love, truly in love this time, and a woman in love will forgive a man almost anything. Her persistent, placating murmurs, spoken in Adam's defense, proved to be as powerful, in their own way, as Dickie's roars.

"No, Uncle Dickie," she said patiently. "You shan't thrash Adam, or throttle him or throw him from the Tyne Bridge. The poor man has twenty stitches in his head. Surely he's suffered enough."

"You listen to me, Nickie—" Dickie began, but Nicole cut him off.

"It's your turn to listen," she told him.

It sounded as if the worst of the storm had blown over, so I tapped on the door and went in.

Claire's portrait had been moved from the bed to the mantelpiece, and Edward's photograph had been tucked into the lower lefthand corner of the portrait's gilded frame. Theirs were the only tranquil faces in the room.

Adam sat slumped against his mound of pillows, his palm cupped gently over his left eye, looking as if his head were about to explode. Dickie stood at the foot of the bed, legs planted wide and arms akimbo, gazing in exasperation at his niece. Nicole was in the visitor's chair, meeting her uncle's gaze with a rather fiery one of her own.

When she saw me, her face lit up.

"Lori!" she exclaimed. "I'm so glad you've come. Adam's told us of the way in which Claire . . . influenced your behavior. I'm so looking forward to telling Guy that he was wrong about you. When his men saw you and Adam up on the moors, he naturally assumed that——"

"I know what he assumed." I ducked my head to hide my blushes. "Doesn't it bother you to know that you've been living with a ghost?"

"I've been living in a house filled with high explosives," Nicole replied. "Compared to that, a single ghost seems almost pleasant."

"Don't forget the thief," Dickie grumbled.

"I haven't." Nicole nailed her uncle with a stern glare. "You listen to me, Uncle Dickie. Wyrdhurst is my home, not yours. It's up to me to decide whether or not to bring charges against Adam, and I choose not to. Adam is a member of my family. My door will always be open to him."

"Doesn't seem to need doors," Dickie muttered.

Nicole sniffed. "If you must be angry with someone, for heaven's sake be angry with Josiah. That evil man's responsible for everything that's happened."

"Ah, well . . ." Dickie's tone became marginally more conciliatory. "I suppose you're right, love. The old devil has a lot to answer for." He cocked a calculating eye at Adam. "I'll wager you think your mother should've been raised a Byrd and given every advantage."

Adam returned his look with one of quiet dignity. "My mother had the greatest advantage of all, sir: a secure and happy childhood. It enabled her to make a great success of her life. She needs neither your pity nor your charity."

Dickie's neck turned red. "I wasn't offering—"

"Nor was I asking," Adam interrupted. "I didn't come here to claim anything from you, not even kinship."

"You wanted to steal the letters," Dickie snapped.

"You wouldn't have missed them," Adam said heatedly. "You didn't even know they existed."

"What the eye doesn't see, the heart doesn't grieve over, eh?" Dickie snarled. "Was that how you planned to justify stealing the treasure?"

"I've told you already," Adam replied through gritted teeth. "I don't know where the treasure is."

"I do."

Two and a half pairs of eyes swung in my direction.

I stepped forward. "I know where the treasure is."

"Don't keep us guessing," Dickie barked. "Where is the bloody thing?"

Nicole made way for me as I crossed to the bedside table. When I pulled a penknife from my pocket and reached for Major Ted, her eyes widened in alarm.

"Minor surgery," I assured her. "He won't feel a thing."

I sat cross-legged on the bed and inserted the knife blade between Teddy's head and the band of his high-peaked officer's hat. With infinite care, I sliced through each neat stitch that held the hat in place, then set the knife aside and lifted the hat from the bear's toffee-colored head. A collective gasp went up as we caught the glint of old gold gleaming from between Teddy's ears.

The rings were set with bloodred rubies in a sumptuous Byzantine filigree. One was large enough for a grown woman, the other meant for a much tinier hand. They were sewn securely to the top of Teddy's head and wedged between them, held in place with an X of silken thread, was a tightly folded square of yellowed paper. When I freed the rings, I passed them to Nicole, but I placed the square of paper in Adam's hand.

He unfolded it delicately, so as not to tear a single crease. A ragged edge suggested that the scrap had been torn from a larger sheet, as if Claire had chosen to preserve only one part of a longer letter. When Adam saw Edward's scrawl, he took a shaky breath, and read aloud:

"'And something to put aside for the daughter we'll have after we're married, my darling, for I pray to God that we'll have no sons. I want no child of mine to roam these battle-fields, except, perhaps, to mourn the men who died here.'"

The fire's crackle and the steady drumming of the rain filled the heavy silence. Edward had written his last words without knowing that his daughter would be born after his death, or that her son would one day roam the battlefields, telling the stories of the men who died there.

Nicole was the first to break the silence. She held the baby ring out to Adam, saying, "Take it."

Adam turned his face away. "I don't want it."

"You'll not get it," Dickie muttered.

"Yes, he will." Nicole pointed to the portrait. "Claire brought us together. She wants us to be one family. Are the two of you too stiff-necked to respect her wishes?"

The men eyed each other resentfully. Finally, Dickie drew himself up and approached the head of the bed, his hand outstretched.

"Just make sure you come through the front door from

now on," he said gruffly. "As Nickie says, it'll always be open to you."

Adam resisted a moment longer before relenting.

Dickie gave his hand a hearty shake, then took the baby ring from Nicole and shoved it under Adam's nose. "Now, young man, you take this ring and give it to your mother. Tell her to come to Wyrdhurst, if she can find the time. Nickie and I would very much like to meet her."

"She'll find the time." Adam took the ring and folded it in the scrap of paper. "She taught me long ago that nothing's more important than family."

A cool breeze caressed my cheek and I looked up at the portrait. The face that had seemed demure in the storeroom and defiant in the library was now entirely at peace. She gazed benevolently down at us, with Edward by her side, secure in the knowledge that their daughter had lived to raise a loving son.

What more, I wondered, could any mother ask?

EPILOGUE

The next day was All Hallows Eve. Nicole assembled us in the library for a ceremony to commemorate the anniversary of Claire's Byrd's birth.

It was hard to believe that only a week had passed since my car had tumbled down the mountainside. As I looked slowly around the room, my gaze moving from one familiar face to the next, I felt a poignant sense of impending loss. The strangers of a week ago had become friends. I'd leave something of myself behind at Wyrdhurst, and hold a place in my heart for each of them when I left.

Adam, wearing his own black jeans and cobalt-blue ribbed sweater, rested in relative comfort on the sofa, while Dickie Byrd fussed with a magnum of champagne. Nicole and Guy stood arm in arm before the hearth, gazing up at Claire.

Hatch had removed the clouded mirror from above the fireplace and replaced it with Claire's portrait. Edward's photograph, framed in silver, sat atop the mantelpiece, beside a delicate glass dome. Beneath the dome, pillowed on a cushion of black velvet, lay the gold-and-ruby ring, the ring that signified a bond that neither a world war nor a father's twisted love could break.

I looked over my shoulder at the empty space above the rolltop desk. At Nicole's behest, Hatch had filled the peepholes and delivered Josiah's portrait to Blackhope's bonfire pile, where it would burn amid much rejoicing on Guy Fawkes Day. Nicole could think of no more fitting punishment for the old devil than to consign his grim image to the flames.

Nicole planned to fill the space with an oil painting she'd commissioned, based on Edward's photograph. Since the library had brought Claire and Edward together, she wanted them to reign over it for as long as Wyrdhurst stood.

The ceremony began with a heartfelt prayer for the repose of all young lovers' souls, and continued with many glasses of Veuve Cliquot. The champagne brought a sparkle to Nicole's eyes and gave her the courage to step forward.

"I know it's a bit premature," she said, "but since it's our last day together, Guy and I wanted you all to know that we'll have a special announcement to make as soon as my present marriage—if one can call it that—is annulled." She blushed prettily as we offered sincere wishes for their happiness. "I'm afraid you'll have to find another tenant for Wyrdhurst, Uncle Dickie. Guy's being transferred to Germany in the spring."

The savvy businessman was unfazed. He'd foreseen

Nicole's departure and mapped out Wyrdhurst's future accordingly. For the next half hour, he regaled us with his plan to turn Josiah's folly into a first-class hotel, with a spacious suite reserved for the family and plenty of jobs for the villagers.

"I'm going to clear Josiah's muck out of the library," he declared, "and replace it with Claire's toys and clothes and books." He gazed levelly at Adam. "We'll call it the Claire Cresswell Museum of Childhood, in honor of Adam's grandparents."

"Claire Cresswell." Adam repeated the name slowly, as if trying it out for the first time, then raised his glass to Dickie. "It's a fine idea, sir."

"Of course it is. I thought of it." Dickie turned to me. "I don't suppose you could persuade Claire to hang about for a bit, could you, Lori?"

"I don't think so," I replied. "Claire doesn't need to be here anymore."

"Well, for God's sake, don't tell anyone that Wyrdhurst isn't haunted," Dickie urged. "There's nothing like a resident ghost to bring the tourists running."

The party began to break up when Dickie, enamored of his new pet project, went off to call various high-powered pals in the hotel industry. A short time later, Nicole and Guy excused themselves to go for a drive up over the moors.

Before he departed, Guy took me aside. "I want to thank you for putting in a good word for me, after Jared left."

"Don't be silly," I chided. "Dickie would have to be as blind as old Josiah not to see that you and Nicole were made for each other."

"Still," he said worriedly, "it must be a bit of a disappointment. Not every millionaire wants his niece to become a soldier's wife."

"This one does." I took him by the arm and turned him to face Edward's photograph. "You're upholding an old family tradition."

Guy's smile, so seldom on display, was as brilliant as the sun and twice as warm. He snapped a salute to Edward and gave me a peck on the cheek before turning to his fiancée.

"Lori," Nicole said. "I don't know how to thank you."

I shrugged. "I wouldn't say no to a lifetime supply of Claire's Lace."

"Done," said Nicole, and enveloped me in a hug.

As they left the library, I could have sworn that the only thing keeping Nicole's feet on the ground was Guy's arm around her waist.

Finally, Adam and I were alone.

As I settled beside him on the sofa, I recalled the first time we'd sat there, when I'd shown him the inscription in *Shuttleworth's Birds* and he'd told me about the young man who'd loved the moors. When I asked if he remembered the exchange, he nodded.

"I'll never forget it," he said "It was the first time I saw words written in Edward's own hand. I can't tell you what it did to me. Those few words brought my grandfather to life."

"That's what you do," I said. "You tell the stories of the men who fought beside him. Your words bring them to life. He'd be so grateful to you."

"No more grateful than I am to him." Adam glanced at the ebony clock. "Your husband should be here soon."

I rolled my eyes. "You'll never believe where he's taking me."

"If it's amusing, I don't want to hear," Adam said sternly. "My ribs are still quite tender."

"We're going to spend a few days in Edinburgh," I said, with a perfectly straight face. "He wants to take in a session of the Scottish Parliament."

Groans mingled with Adam's laughter. He breathed shallowly for a moment, then reached out to take my hand. "You're a sadist, Lori Shepherd. I can't imagine why I ever thought your husband the most fortunate of men."

I squeezed his hand. "Must be the concussion."

Adam opened his mouth to reply, then closed it abruptly. "Lori," he said, peering past my shoulder, "am I seeing things?"

I turned to follow his gaze. The ruby ring still lay on its velvet cushion beneath the delicate glass dome, but its twin was now in the portrait, adorning the third finger of Claire's left hand.

"Is it the concussion?" Adam asked. "Or too much champagne?"

"I'd say it calls for more champagne." I seized the bottle. "Don't you get it? They've finally said their vows."

Adam eyed me doubtfully. "Will anyone else be able to see it?"

"Are you kidding?" I refilled his glass and mine. "*Everyone* will. Claire's been wanting to show off that ring for a long time."

"Dear Lord," Adam said faintly. "I can see Dickie's adverts now. He'll sell Wyrdhurst rings in the gift shop."

"Along with Claire-and-Edward T-shirts . . ."

". . . and tins of Claire's Lace . . ."

". . . and military teddies . . ."

". . . and miniature models of the Devil's Ring. Oh, my poor ribs," Adam said, wincing as he chuckled. "Wyrdhurst will never be the same."

Wyrdhurst would never be the same, I thought, and that wasn't such a bad thing. For nearly a hundred years the house had enshrined a painful past. It was time to clear its corridors of cobwebs, throw open its hidden doors, take the bars from its windows, and fill its neglected garden with color and scent.

The ghosts of Wyrdhurst's past had been laid to rest. Its future was with the living.

∽ Claire's Lace ∽

1 cup sifted flour
1 cup chopped flaked coconut or
     chopped walnuts
½ cup light corn syrup
½ cup firmly packed brown sugar
½ cup butter or margarine
1 teaspoon vanilla

PREHEAT OVEN TO 350 DEGREES.

Mix flour and coconut (or walnuts).

Combine light corn syrup, brown sugar, and butter or margarine in heavy saucepan. Over medium heat, bring syrup mixture to boil, stirring constantly. Remove from heat.

Gradually blend flour mixture, then vanilla, into syrup mixture.

Drop onto foil-covered cookie sheets by scant teaspoonfuls, 3 inches apart (dough will spread during baking). Bake for 8–10 minutes.

Cool on wire rack until foil peels easily. Remove foil. Place cookies on rack covered with absorbent paper.

Yield: four dozen cookies